I0621799

DEADLY

INTENT

Kate Allenton

Published by Coastal Escape Publishing

Discover other titles by Kate Allenton

At http://www.kateallenton.com

DEADLY INTENT

ISBN-10:

1-944237-27-5

ISBN-13:

978-1-944237-27-1

DEDICATION

This book is dedicated to my sister, Vicki, because sometimes parkas are really needed in Florida.

And to

My fabulous cousins.

Natalie, Suzanne, Cindy, and Lorenna, you guys always make our family get-together's so much fun. Grab your sunblock and let the husbands watch the kids. This beach read is for each of you. #NewSmyrna2016 or bust.

ACKNOWLEDGMENTS

This book would not be in existence without the love and support of my family and friends who gave me the gentle nudge needed to see this through. Thank you. I appreciate each and every one of you

Chapter 1

Most people would find it odd walking into their house, after a long day at work, to find a ghost poking his head inside a closed fridge. Quinn Thatcher wasn't most people.

"Don't be sliming all over my leftover Chinese noodles, Clarence," she scolded while tossing her purse and keys onto the bar.

"You're going to die from clogged arteries. There isnae a vegetable in your house, and as you well know, we donae *ooze slime* like in the movies."

Quinn knew a lot about ghosts, and she should; it was her job. Yet she

1

couldn't help aggravating the uppity Scottish Highlander who had decided to haunt her day and night until she listened to his problems. The ghost was slowly learning she was even more stubborn than the leather pants in her closet that refused to budge over her hips. She, too, was unwilling to give that extra inch or three.

"Don't you have some family members you'd rather haunt?"

"I donae."

She sighed, left the food voyeur in the kitchen, and went to change her clothes and ditch her bra. The ghost wasn't going to stop her from getting comfortable in her own home. Returning a few minutes later, she pulled her hair up into a ponytail.

"I can give you the addresses of a few people who deserve a good scare. Have you learned to rattle chains yet?"

His sigh of aggravation made her chuckle. She had this innate ability to bring out the best in everyone. Ghosts were no exception.

"Lass, I'll leave when you help me."

If only that were true. Quinn had been duped once by a little old lady who worried about who was going to take care of her ten cats. Never again.

"You shouldn't have invaded my private space. I might have considered it."

Quinn grabbed a pint of chunky monkey from the freezer and a spoon before turning on *Gone with the Wind*. The movie worked like ghost repellant; most disappeared before the opening credits.

"You're gonna make me do this the hard way, aren't ya, lass?"

"Give me your worst." Quinn grinned while turning up the TV volume.

"So be it."

Quinn's mother had always warned her to be careful what she asked for. She was about to find out exactly which one was more stubborn—the Scottish ghost or southern medium.

Rest in Peace would never be inscribed on her gravestone, like the one she was sitting on top of. Nor would the attendees cry a tear once she kicked the bucket. Her death would never be from natural causes, more like from falling off a table while dancing topless as she belted out the wrong lyrics to her favorite song. It could happen. It almost had.

Both men and women wanted to strangle her for her unusual manner and razor-sharp tongue. One had already tried and failed miserably. The poor shmuck was serving ten in the state pen after a spirit convinced her that the perp was responsible for his early demise. Maybe she shouldn't have confronted him alone.

She wasn't a cop; she didn't carry a badge, and she didn't solve crimes. Her contribution was a little more on the down-low and usually swept under the rug. Police agencies would never admit to using her skills, and she couldn't blame them. How was she supposed to prove what she saw in her head?

Conversing with the dead was much more entertaining than conversing with the living. It was a gift and a curse, one she acknowledged proudly, like the red tangled curls on her head, which had lost their luster in the choking humidity and eerily strange wind while sitting in the cemetery. Gathering the strands, she pulled them back with the ponytail holder she kept on her wrist for just this purpose, and the occasional infliction of red marks on people she didn't like.

Her only company lay entombed in a steel casket six feet beneath her feet. Darkness cloaked her in the graveyard; not even the moon was on her side. She wasn't scared of waiting in the sacred place alone. Just the opposite.

Ghosts didn't tend to hang around their final resting place, no matter what the living thought. She'd often tell her clients, if they wanted to talk to their deceased loved ones, to save the gas and do it in the comfort of their homes.

Chances were good that their relatives were already visiting.

The scent of roses drifted to her nose. Conversation from approaching voices pierced her peace. She didn't need to turn around to know her sisters had arrived. Their laughter could wake the dead.

"You're all late," she called out and hopped down off the cool marble stone, giving her bony butt a break. Steven Simmons would be pleased she was no longer sitting on his face.

"This place is creepy. I don't know why we can't meet at the office like normal people," Becca called out as she approached. She shivered, rubbing her wool-covered arms. It didn't matter that Becca was a native Floridian, living on the Redneck Riviera where the words ya'll and drunken spring breakers were as normal as wearing flip-flops all year round in ninety-degree weather. Becca was in dire need of a supersized value meal to help her achieve another layer of fat to keep her warm.

Sometimes Quinn wondered whether Becca was really blood related and not the product of a secret affair between their mother and the butler. She shook her head. Regardless of Becca's heritage and love for green vegetables, Quinn loved her.

"We get paid for creepy," she reminded her.

"Tell me again why we're here," Quinn's other sister, Cara, said while peering down at the stone in front of her. Her lips twisted into a frown as she touched the old cracked marble. Quinn's butt wasn't responsible for that particular crack. Cara's ability was different from the rest of family that could see ghosts. One touch of anything personal, or emotionally charged by the dead, and she could see the spirit's life flash before her eyes. Why anyone would need that ability was a mystery.

Quinn loved her sisters, all four of them, although sometimes they were the reason she enjoyed playing with the dead over the living.

"Where are Harper and Grace?" she asked impatiently, folding her arms over the big red lips printed on her shirt.

Cara yanked her hand to her chest and rubbed her palm. "They're still out of town working in New Orleans. You'd know that if you actually showed up to our meetings."

Well, if that news didn't bite a big donkey butt. Those two officially couldn't be persuaded by Quinn's manipulative plan if they weren't even in town. There would be another time for them. "Clarence finally wore me down but refuses to shimmer out of my life."

Both of her sisters' eyes widened, and they remained speechless. Quinn wasn't surprised by their reaction. It took a lot to break her resolve. She'd ignored him for a solid month.

Last night, he'd breached her personal sanctuary, entering her bathroom during shower karaoke.

Quinn slipped her fingers into her pocket and slid out the reason for his constant badgering. A heart-shaped emerald, the size of her fist, dangled from a sturdy gold chain. The gem remained freezing to the touch, as if it had been hidden in the gallon carton of chunky monkey in her freezer instead of in a metal box buried next to Clarence's headstone.

"Oh my God." Cara lifted the heart into her palms. "This is real."

"As real as my breast," Quinn proudly announced after hours of research online, not taking Clarence at his word. She should have. It would have saved her time. "It's an heirloom piece that belongs to the Menzie clan in Scotland."

Cara yanked back her hand and pointed an accusing finger at the gem. "That thing is cursed. You need to put it back where you found it."

"And risk Clarence becoming a permanent haunt in my life?" Quinn shook her head vehemently. "No can do, Cara. You must be smoking some good shit, and I'm kind of offended you aren't sharing, but there is no way in hell that opera-singing wannabe is keeping me up at night for the rest of my life. Have you ever heard a Scottish ghost try opera?" Quinn's entire body cringed at the memory of last night's performance. The sound was as loud and annoying as a foghorn mating with a tornado siren.

"Maybe you should listen to her," Becca suggested.

Bless her heart. She was still so young and naïve. "My research indicated that there are two clans still feuding over this little gem, Becca. Aren't you the one who cares about world peace and love? I thought for sure that you'd be on my side."

"We're not going, and you shouldn't either. I won't touch that thing again, and Becca....she isn't prepared enough to deal with the spirits in Scotland." Cara slipped her arm around Becca's as if Quinn was about to play a game of tug of war. The thought had crossed her mind.

Traitors. Quinn should be fuming and seeing red, but she was as proud of her baby sisters showing their claws like a mother bird watching her babies take flight.

"If that's how you want to be, then fine." Quinn waved the fortune in her hand. "If there's any commission, then I'm keeping it, but regardless, this is my one shot to ditch Clarence, so I'm out of here." She spun in her Converses and stalked away. "And I'm taking one of Daddy's jets and charging it to the company." No way in hell would she be tortured in cramped spaces with crying babies or worse. She had hours of sleep to make up for, thanks to Clarence. Get there, give them the jewelry, and then hightail it home and pray that Clarence shimmered from sight.

Chapter 2

A gush of cold air blew up Quinn's skirt as she exited the plane. It reminded her of the famous picture of Marilyn Monroe, only her legs weren't as slim and she had a lot more junk in her trunk. Other than that, they were practically twins from the neck down. Quinn rubbed her bare arms, trying to restore blood flow. Her sister's wool parka wasn't so funny now.

Johnny Smith, the family pilot, stepped out of the cockpit. His normally tan face was pale and held a tinge of green. Beads of sweat didn't just dot his brow, they ran down like ice cream in a small child's hand in the Florida heat.

"Are you okay?"

He nodded seconds before launching his lunch over the stair railing. The white chunks and green liquid made her stomach roll. Chicken and split pea soup. The nice thing to do would have been to rub his back in comfort, but she wasn't nice. Instead of getting closer, she stepped back and covered her mouth with her hand, trying to ignore the retching sounds. No, no, no, she wasn't getting sick in some godforsaken foreign town that probably didn't even have a real doctor.

"I must have had a reaction to the food," Johnny said, leaning back inside the plane and grabbing a towel for his mouth.

Sure. He had *something* all right.

"You're my ride home. We need to get you to bed and get you better." Quinn shivered and took his arm to help him wobble down the stairs and into the private terminal. Her skirt fluttered against her skin, giving the ground crew a free peep of her big white moon and matching-color G-string. Pervs. At least her legs were tan. "You need sleep."

Not to mention a gallon of mouthwash and a toothbrush.

Outside the empty terminal, an old white-haired man stood in front of the black Town Car holding a cardboard sign with Quinn's last name scribbled in a child's handwriting. The fine lines around his mouth showed years of laughter. Warmth and knowledge sparkled in the depth of his blue eyes, the same shade as her favorite faded blue jeans.

"I'd like to check in at the hotel first please and then be taken to the Menzie castle." She used her best southern charm. Johnny was no help, so she grabbed his bag and hers and helped load them both into the trunk while Johnny slipped inside the car.

"My name's Angus. I'll be your driver during your stay."

Quinn shook his hand. "I'm Quinn Thatcher. It's nice to meet you." Her mother would be pleased she hadn't rolled her eyes and just gotten in the car. Her mom was a true southern belle who had married into old money, but she'd never been one of those stuck-up snobs, like some of her chicken-legged friends. Her mom had taught her girls to be just as pleasing. Quinn's pleasing side could use some work.

"Aye, what brings you to our fair town?"

"Business." She smiled politely like her momma had taught her and had been just as vague as dear old dad when mom questioned him about his late-night drunken escapades.

"Where's the rest of your things?"

"That's everything. We're only staying overnight." Quinn crossed her fingers, hoping what she said was true.

The limo lurched; Johnny's hand flew to cover his mouth, and Quinn unceremoniously bonked her head against the seat back. Did Scotland even require driver's licenses?

"Sorry, lass. We donae drive much around these parts. We prefer horses."

Oh for the love of God. Quinn silently held her tongue, wondering if every passing mile was taking her a decade back in history.

Johnny settled into his own room, and Quinn left him with medicine and water before heading to the castle. The emerald sat heavy against her chest as her sister's words about a curse entered her mind. Angus drove out of the small quaint town, giving her a picturesque view of heather growing freely in a multitude of purple hues over the passing farmlands. Her nose twitched in anticipation of her upcoming allergy attack. No matter how beautiful flowers were, being within ten feet of them started a sneezing fest that would leave her puffy and red for days.

Angus pulled down a long driveway and stopped. The stone castle loomed up into the sky. Construction workers scurried around the scaffolding against the one side of the building. Curse, shmurse. The owner wasn't hurting.

A ghost dressed in a blue dress stood in one of the towers, looking down. "Uh-uh, I'm not here to deal with you. It's my day off, lady."

"Excuse me?" Angus asked.

"Just talking to myself. Ignore me." Quinn issued her standard answer for the times when she knew she sounded mad. Maybe she was. Regardless, no one had proof...yet.

She slipped out of the car, not waiting for Angus to open her door. His feeble legs looked as though they could use the break. She ducked back inside before shutting the door. "Hopefully, I'll just be a minute."

"I'll wait as long as you need, lass. I'm in no rush to get back to my wife's long list of chores."

"Thanks." Quinn shut the door and drew in a deep breath. Inhaling the nearby ocean air made her feel a little more like home minus the huge jagged cliffs. Returning the stone had been a brilliant idea back in the States. A means to an end to get rid of Clarence, but explaining how she'd found it might take a little finesse. She hoped she'd remembered to pack hers.

Quinn rattled the door knocker to announce her presence. Within seconds, the door flew open and a young maid in full uniform gasped rather loudly and rudely, covering her mouth with her hand. Blood drained from her face, leaving her cheeks as white as her apron.

Maybe Quinn should have checked her hair before getting out of the car. She didn't normally get that type of reaction. "I'm here to see Laird Menzie."

"As I live and breathe, I must be dreaming." The woman gasped again while pinching Quinn's arm.

"Oww, is that your normal greeting?" Quinn pinched her back for good measure. The sting must have triggered some common sense because it brought a little color to the maid's cheeks. They flushed a bright red as she rubbed her arms.

"Excuse me, miss. I'm so sorry. I thought you were a ghost."

Ghost, yes...because everyone could see them. If only that were the case. Quinn might be out of a job, but she'd have a lot more free time. "Sorry to disappoint you. Is the laird around? I really need to speak with him."

A tight smile slipped onto her lips. "He's just up the ridge, and he'll be there most of the day." She pointed toward the hill. "Would you like me to take a message?"

"No, thank you." How did one go about leaving a message that she'd found his green rock? Great. Up a ridge. Quinn glanced down at her stilettos. Perfect. "So if I head up that way, I'll run into him?"

Getting information from this chick was like trying to dig a splinter out from underneath her skin, a sliver of annoyance but necessary.

"Aye, yes, miss. Up the ridge and over the bridge. You cannae miss the lot of them."

The lot of them. It sounded as if Quinn would have an audience for her explanation. Could her day get any better? She waved and stepped down the stairs. "I'll go find him myself."

"I donae think that's wise, miss." Her voice was strained with a mixture of worry and amusement. "He's likely to have the same reaction."

"Don't worry. I'll pinch him too." Quinn, refusing to be dissuaded from her quest, wiggled her fingers and left the maid standing at the door.

Quinn started the climb up the grassy hill. With each step, her perfect white heels sank further into the brown dirt and her calves screamed in protest.

"I could be on the beach working on my tan," she grumbled as Clarence appeared at her side. "Nice of you to show. I hope you're happy and decide to stay."

The damn ghost had the nerve to disappear again. Jerk. If she ever figured out a way to blast ghosts into the light, her job would be easier. She gave up trying to climb the mountain on her tippy-toes to avoid completely ruining her shoes. She slipped them off her feet and dangled them between her fingers as she walked barefoot the rest of the way to the top. Ridge her butt. A baby Mt. Everest was more like it. Okay, so maybe cheeseburgers weren't her friend either.

She heard shouting that got louder as she neared the stone bridge. She crossed it to find several grown men and women standing in a circle. Their plaid clothes reminded her of a picnic without food. Two kilted men sat tall on horseback, one on a black stallion and the other white, while clanking their swords together, making her ears ring. One of the horses rose on his hind legs, and the rider lifted the shiny silver sword in the air and waved it around, like Quinn had while trying to get a male stripper's attention by flashing a twenty-dollar bill. His hooves landed with a thud against the ground, and a ghastly smell permeated the air. Did horses fart? Or maybe it had been the rider. Whoever was responsible, the smell reeked of bad eggs. Quinn stood unsure and stunned as she watched. Taking a tentative step toward the crowd, she held her breath from the smell. Using her shoulders and elbows, she slipped into the surrounding crowd for a better view of the barbaric fight.

"What gives?"

The burly man standing next to her answered without looking in her direction. "The annual reenactment of the Menzie/McDougall battle over the lost emerald. It's tradition."

"I bet." Her lips twitched in amusement. "Which one is Menzie?"

"Menzie is in the green. McDougall is red."

Menzie's arm muscles constricted as he swung his sharp sword, clanging it against his opponent's. A mischievous smile spread across his lips as his eyes twinkled. He was handsome in a rugged kind of way, and she silently wondered if he was all brawn and no brains. She should be so lucky.

Quinn stepped into the arena and held up her arms to stop the battle. "Excuse me..."

The swords continued to clink, and her presence went ignored, so she did what any southern woman would do. She slipped her fingers into her mouth and let out a loud whistle that would have made her mother cringe and her father think he'd raised a tomboy.

Both men came to an abrupt stop and turned their horses in her direction. Both had that...who-the-hell-do-you-think-you-are glare Quinn seemed to get everywhere she went. She rolled her eyes.

People in the crowd gasped with the same greeting as the maid. As long as they kept their pinchers to themselves, no one would get hurt.

Quinn slipped the emerald from around her neck and tossed it toward the man in the green kilt. "Game over. The mighty emerald has been returned. You can each go back to your castles and have a beer or whatever it is you do to celebrate." She planned to.

Quinn smiled brightly and spun on her bare feet, ready to walk away. Within seconds, the sound of galloping hooves and the bark of a dog had her spinning around just as a huge ball of white fur leaped from the ground and tackled her. Her body hit the grass with a thump as a pink tongue licked the length of her cheek, covering her in drool and ruining her makeup. Of course, a psychotic dog. She should have known.

"Harness, heel," a deep-timbered voice boomed with authority from above.

The dog gave her one last lick and climbed off. Crazy mutt. Harness sat on his haunches, staring at Quinn through the white hair that covered his face. His tongue lolled out as he panted, as though waiting to lick her like his favorite lollipop flavor while humping her leg. Quinn's nose twitched while picking the dog hair off her shirt, trying her best to hold in the sneeze that teased for release. A shiver of annoyance traveled down her spine, in a clutching hold, like the flu that had attacked her pilot.

"Good dog," she mumbled, getting back to her feet. She swiped at the dirt stains covering her ruined white skirt. These people could keep their motherland. Scotland and Quinn would never get along.

"Who are you?" Menzie asked, hopping down off his extremely large, white horse. A shame. The wind kept his kilt down. It would have answered an age-old question and brought a whole new meaning to the word bareback. She shivered. Becca would have loved this place, and the knight in shining armor this guy portrayed. Pity that Quinn couldn't have manipulated her to deliver the damn gem.

"I'm nobody, and I'm just leaving." She grabbed her shoes.

"No, wait." His voice held more of a demand than a request. She ignored him. There was only one man that she'd *consider* stopping for when he issued a command, and she called him Dad.

"There isn't enough sinus medicine in all your land to get me to stay," she called over her shoulder and lifted the heels in her hand as a wave goodbye. "Peace, love, and God save the Queen." Was that right? Probably not, but it still brought a genuine smile to her lips.

Laughter and voices continued behind her. The quicker she got back to the hotel, the closer she'd be to getting home.

Quinn had just cleared the bridge when the dog appeared by her side. "Go away. Shoo." She waved her shoes toward him. Her scare tactic bombed, and he rubbed against her leg.

"I'm not here for you," Quinn yelled out to the ghostly woman watching from her perch in the tower. Sometimes ghosts could be as nervous as a long-tailed cat in a room full of rocking chairs, and other times just plain mean. No two were ever the same.

"Who are you talking to, luv?"

Quinn refrained from rolling her eyes as Menzie appeared on her right and McDougall on her left.

"I didn't mean to interrupt your play time. I just wanted to return your prize." She quickened her step. For every two of hers, they took one.

A beefy hand clenched Quinn's arm. The thick fingers dug into her poor delicate skin and she stopped on the spot, adjusting a shoe in each hand with the sharp, pointy heels to use as makeshift weapons. "Remove your hand, or I'm going to find out if you are actually wearing underwear under your skirt when I kick your balls."

"McDougall, release her," Menzie growled, and McDougall smirked. Wrong move. Men were all the same, no matter what country they were from. They'd test her resolve until she shoved it in their faces.

"No, I willnae until the wee lass tells me how she came to find the stone."

"Suit yourself." Quinn slammed both of her heels into his arm and spun, kicking beneath his skirt. Her foot came in contact with sweaty balls. Lucky for him, her newfound anger held her gag reflex at bay. Otherwise, he'd be covered in the same color as his enemy. Green split pea soup.

Mr. McNotSoStudlyNow fell instantly to the ground, cupping his crown jewels. She shrugged.

"Can't say I didn't warn you. You should really think about wearing underwear. I'm not sure it's sanitary for the horses." Much less her foot. She chuckled and continued walking, leaving the Scottish douche on the ground, moaning like a big baby while she desperately tried to remember if she'd packed a bottle of disinfectant in her bag.

"You're a feisty one." Menzie chuckled. "But he deserved it."

"And more. My momma always told me to act like a lady, unless some schmuck tried to treat me like a piece of meat."

"Wise advice," he said as they approached the car, where Angus was waiting with the door open. A smile split his lips, and his eyes twinkled in approval.

"I would say it's been a pleasure, but it hasn't. Good day, Laird Menzie. I hope you have a long life with your prize."

"Who are you?"

She let out a resigned sigh. "Quinn Thatcher. You have your emerald, so my work here is done." She patted the large muscles on his sweaty, bare, tanned chest. Yes, okay, she copped a feel. It was the least he could put up with to repay her for her hell of Mr. Grabby and the obnoxious ghost. "Have a nice life."

"Wait." He reached for her arm. She raised a brow in challenge, making him pause in midair before returning the currently uninjured hand to his side. She'd guessed wrong. This one did have brains. He smiled warmly down at her; his ruggedly handsome face made the butterflies in her stomach flutter to life. "Where did you find the emerald?"

"At the grave of Clarence McNolte in Florida." Quinn slipped inside the car, and Angus shut the door before he could ask more questions she wouldn't be able to answer. Menzie exchanging a few words with Angus before climbing in behind the wheel.

"I must say, lass. Only a strong woman would dare bring a McDougall to his knees."

More like his ass, but she didn't correct Angus. She met his aged eyes in the rearview mirror. "Low blood sugar makes me cranky, and his momma should have taught him better manners."

"Where to?"

"The hotel so I can shower and change." Before her foot turned green and fell off from some sexually transmitted disease, but she kept that comment to herself. When in Rome, it was probably better not to piss off all the natives. "Then I'm getting dinner and a beer at the pub. I won't need the car again today."

"Aye. Sounds like a fine plan."

Fine was an understatement. Quinn leaned back into the seat; the worn leather creaked in protest. Resting her hand over the flutters in her stomach, she pondered whether she'd done the right thing by taking this trip.

Chapter 3

Collin Menzie stared down the driveway and watched Angus drive the redhead away. The legend had been true. Criminy. He was sure that the legend had been a lie, perpetrated by whoever had stolen the stone. The cool breeze that he'd enjoyed earlier carassed his skin but didn't stop the blood from boiling in his veins. Why had he been the one to be saddled with the legend and not an ancestor before?

"Looks like the emerald has returned, and under my watch." McDougall chuckled as he slapped Collin's back. "If the story stands true, the jewel shall finally find its final resting place among my colors *and* on her finger."

With friends like Ian McDougall, a man didn't need enemies. The old wives' tale foretold that a member of the Menzie clan would wed with a part of the stone before handing it back to a McDougall. Not likely since it had been a peace offering from the McDougall clan to the Menzies, not to mention the thought of putting a ring on the American's finger. His fate was his own, no matter what the gypsy had proclaimed.

"Care to consult the paintings to get a fresh perspective of what to expect."

The infamous paintings depicted a tale of what to expect in the coming days. The so called Savior was among them who'd be changing Collin's life forever.

"Aye." Collin spun to find the entire staff waiting. Each held a worried look in their eyes and rightly so. The legend coming to life, and the omen that followed wasn't something any smart man would ignore. Disease, death, fire, and ruin were eminent if the old tales were to be believed.

"If I were you, I'd have Ramsey hide your gold and monitor the accounts."

It had been years since Collin had studied the text and the paintings. He'd laughed it off as a cocky young lad, convinced no imaginary redhead from the curse would ever get the best of him. Had he been wrong all these years?

"Shows over." Collin clapped his hands, dispersing the crowd to lead Ian inside the castle. The thud of the heavy doors reverberated through the hall as the doors shut behind them. Ian and Collin had been raised by their fathers to hate each other, but the opposite had happened when Ian returned Collin's favorite horse, which had taken off from the first of many fires. He'd since been one of the few souls that Collin trusted, along with Ramsey, Collin's accountant.

Collin had no more than cleared the door when Margarete came rushing forward. Her enthusiasm about furniture and décor wasn't the only thing she wanted within these walls. Many a night Collin had brushed off her advances, but it appeared as though she had some crazy inner radar to know when he was home. "Collin. We must talk about the tapestries."

Margarete was a beautiful woman in her own right. She was educated and held a regal air of title in the way she presented herself. She was slender with blonde hair and a stick-straight figure. Many a man would have been proud if she showed them attention. Collin wasn't one of them. Her beauty did little to hide her pretentious attitude toward the staff. He'd hired her due to her eye for detail ininterior decorating. He hadn't been expecting her to turn her eyes to him. He should have known.

"No, wench, we have much more pressing matters to discuss," Ian complained.

"What your brother meant to say was, can it wait?" Collin asked, trying hard to soften Ian's words.

"Sure." Her cheeks flushed pink, and she pasted a hardened smile on her face and lifted her chin. Whenever Ian visited, he managed to piss off everyone in his path, whether he intended to or not. He'd turned his brash attitude into a game of sport to flirt with the women he encountered. He had a way with words and with women. More than one of the maids had been found in a closet with her skirt up to her chest. Ian was truly gifted in the art of seduction.

Having Margarete beneath Collin's roof seemed to only make things worse. It was as though her presence alone managed to set the staff's nerves on edge with her constant demands, as if she were the lady of the castle. Hiring her had been a favor; keeping her content had been the challenge. She was here to do a job, one that Collin had no desire to perform, and Ian's rudeness always seemed to aggravate her more. Restoring and redecorating the part of the castle that had succumbed to fire wasn't Collin's idea of a good time. Ever.

He led the way up the north tower where Gwinnie's ghost was reportedly lingering. He didn't believe in such nonsense. Her ghost had never appeared to him, and he was related by blood. She'd been a new daughter-in-law in the household all those years ago when the emerald had vanished. It was her mother-in-law, Lady Menzie, who had commissioned the gypsy to paint, based off what the crazy gypsy woman saw in her visions. *Not so crazy now*, Collin thought.

Using his shoulder, he shimmied open the jammed door to one of the few rooms in the castle that the staff avoided at all cost. The solid wood flew open, slamming into the wall as if an unseen restraint had been removed. Dust floated in the sunshine coming through the windows that surrounded the empty room. The paintings had hung in the ballroom as a constant reminder of things to come, until Margarete had started redecorating. She'd stored them in the tower where they were leaning against the wall and covered in old sheets. Ian and Collin removed all of the coverings before standing in complete silence, staring at the painting of a woman who looked like Quinn Thatcher. The resemblance was uncanny, down to the freckles he'd noticed on her neck.

Collin rubbed the stubble on his chin, trying to remember the story that accompanied the paintings. He shouldn't have bothered. Ian knew the first few lines word for word.

"A woman with hair of fire, and eyes the color of the stolen stone, will descend from the sky."

Collin's lips twisted into a nervous smile. Her eyes were the first thing he'd noticed before his gaze lowered to the generous curves of her body and breasts. The mysterious woman was a beauty.

"Her word will carry a bite and sting worse than the fiercest beast."

"Nailed that one," Collin grumbled, much to his dismay. She wasn't timid by any stretch of the imagination, if her actions portrayed her personality. She'd sauntered into the middle of a fight, commanded attention and had managed to bring Ian to his knees. Stronger men had tried and failed.

"Making the lines of past and present blur," Ian continued.

"What do you suppose that means?"

Ian shrugged.

"What was the rest?"

"Disease will spread; death will follow; walls will crumble, and men will fall."

"She's already conquered taking down a man. I suggest you try not to manhandle her, like your other women, until we know what's going on." Collin ignored the need to lay a protective hand over his own balls, remembering Quinn's determination. Pissing her off should be avoided at all cost.

"Friend or foe, it is she who controls the Menzie destiny, and will bring down the deceit of once noble men, making them fall from grace into hell," Ian said, repeating the last verse of the tale.

Collin ran his hand through his hair, ignoring the other paintings, and moved to the window to look out over the vast land. On most days, the view of heather-covered braes bathed in sunlight and the distant view of the ocean managed to bring peace to his soul. Today wasn't one of those days. An unease he couldn't explain settled into his bones. A warning of things yet to pass.

"Friend or foe, she controls your destiny. What are you going to do?" Ian asked as Collin rubbed at the stubble on his chin. That was the million-dollar question. What was he going to do? He could ignore her, and hope she went away, or press for answers in an attempt to resolve the legend once and for all.

"I guess I donae have a choice," Collin answered, spinning around. "I'll go find her and see what else she might know."

"Are you sure the lass is still here?"

"Aye. Angus told me she's staying until the morn."

"Well, she's got to eat, and we both know they donae serve food at the hotel. It should be easy enough for us to track her down."

"Go get cleaned up, and I'll meet you at the pub in an hour."

A plan formed in Collin's head, one that had Quinn Thatcher singing like a canary. Not many women could withstand his charm, but he had a feeling she might be the first. Leading the way out of the old room, Collin walked Ian out of the castle, not giving him any time to pick his next conquest. Stopping in the study, Collin grabbed his cell phone before returning to the north tower. He snapped a picture of the painting to compare face to face. The lass would need proof if she were to believe a word he said.

Chapter 4

After being dropped off, Quinn hit a small boutique filled with flannel and boots. Thirty minutes later, she walked out wearing a red plaid lumberjack-looking shirt and even thicker jacket. The added layers hid her soft curves but kept her warm. She sighed at the lengths she was willing to go to help Clarence resolve his issues.

The warmer clothes and shower did wonders for her mood as she sat patiently inside the pub next door waiting on her order of fish and chips to arrive. She sipped a pint of light colored beer. The bitter ale coated her tongue and slid down her throat with ease. The request for a Miller Lite had gone ignored. Pizza and burgers were not on the menu, sealing

Quinn's resolve to cross this vacation spot off her list. A noxious smell came from the kitchen that made her stomach roll, and she wondered if it was haggis, the main dish that Scotland was so famous for pushing on unsuspecting tourist. A prior internet search had saved her from her upchuck reflux.

A group of old timers surrounded a table, engaged in lively debate. A few patrons sat farther down the bar, and the atmosphere was friendly and ghost-free. She hadn't known what to expect when she walked into the pub, but an impending unease left her gut churning. It could have easily been from her empty-stomach alcohol buzz.

Scotland was rumored to be overflowing with ancient ghosts. Either they were playing a good game of hide and seek, or they just disliked haunting the tourists. Quinn closed her eyes, thankful for the brief reprieve. The angry glare from the female ghost in the castle tower remained tattooed behind her lids, forever branded into Quinn's mind like the look on her baby sister's face when she caught Quinn trying to feed her goldfish to her pet parakeet.

A man slid onto the bar stool to Quinn's right and another one on her left. The two big bodies squished her arms into her sides. She dropped her head and gave an aggravating shake. Of all the stools, in all the pubs, these two just ended up next to her.

"A simple thank you would have sufficed."

Karma was a funny bitch, and it appeared Quinn had a target stamped on her forehead in flashing neon green that read...Bring...It...On.

She opened her eyes and recognized the beefy fingers from earlier, only now they weren't attached to her arm but holding out some bills toward the bartender.

"Sorry about earlier, lass," McDougall grumbled as if the apology pained him. Inflicting more crossed her mind.

Her hearing was perfect, and his apology was worse than a child's with his momma pinching his ear and holding him in place, ready to whip his ass if he didn't say the words with sincerity. Quinn smiled down into her beer. "Come again? I don't think I heard you."

"You heard me," he barked.

"Touch me again like that and I can promise much worse." Had Quinn's father been here, they would have high-fived. Well, whatever it was that men with class did these days. Maybe raised a bourbon in salute. She wouldn't know. The last time she'd spoken to him was to announce the formation of Linked Inc., the psychic business she'd started with her sisters. Now she just tried to stay away from her parents as much as possible. Not that she didn't love them, but the backlash from forming the business had caused the family a bit of criticism.

"Forgive Ian. We were both shocked that you had solved a century-old puzzle," Menzie said as the bartender placed darker beers in front of both of the guys. "We dinnae formally introduce ourselves. He's Ian McDougall, and I'm Collin Menzie."

"That's great. Enjoy your evening." Quinn slid off her stool, grabbed her oversized coat, and picked up her beer before motioning to the bartender she was moving to a table across the room.

The two big oafs ignored the hint and followed. If she could figure out the come-hither vibes she didn't realize she was sending, she'd bottle that shit up and sell it because she hadn't extended invitations to either man. Each of them took a chair at her newly acquired table. "The missing gem is returned, and your family peace is restored. Why are you following me?"

"I thought Yanks were hospitable," Ian grumbled over the rim of his pint.

"And I thought all things in Scotland were bigger than in America." Quinn glanced down into Ian's lap. "Clearly we've both been misled." She lied. Ian had plenty of manhood to impress women. But one rude comment deserved another. *Why am I letting him get to me?*

Ian slammed his fist against the table and rose to his full height. He glared at her with his hazel eyes while running a hand through his dirty blond hair.

"Relax, stud. I was teasing."

"Collin, control your wench," Ian said, returning to his seat.

Quinn snapped her gaze to the aggravating Highlander and clenched her fingers around her mug while she pondered if she had enough cash in her wallet to make bail. "Wench?"

"He calls every beautiful woman a wench," Collin said, resting his palm on her arm. "Careful, Quinn. He likes challenge in his conquests, and you might be next on his list."

"I knew I should have just mailed the damn thing. Is this part of the curse? You follow the do-gooder and harass her?" She was restless and irritable; her voice sounded hoarse with tired frustration.

"You know about the curse?" Collin's eyes grew large as his lips turned down at the corners.

Ian spewed his beer and started in a coughing fit, making Quinn smile. She raised her beer. "If you can't handle your booze, you shouldn't drink, studly."

Ian swiped the back of his hand against his mouth. "What do *you* know of the curse?"

"Enough to know there is one." She took a sip of her beer, watching a range of emotions roll across Collin's face. His brows dipped in concern as the blues in his eyes swirled and darkened to that of an impending thunderstorm. The bar grew silent as if the other occupants understood the nature of their conversation and were eavesdropping, waiting for answers.

A genuine smile grew on Quinn's face as she spotted the approaching bartender with her fish and chips. *Finally, sustenance.* The Miller Lite debacle was forgotten and forgiven like her nagging sister's lecture about flying to Scotland. "You're a God among men."

Her words earned her a wink and a sexy smile. Men were so easy.

The Highlanders at the table stayed pleasantly silent, so she let them stew and studied her food. What Scots called chips were what Americans called fries. The fried greasy goodness made her mouth salivate in anticipation. She popped one in her mouth and moaned in bliss.

"How did you find out about the curse?" Collin asked with quiet but resolute firmness. His playful features and handsome smile had turned into something more of a hardened man demanding answers. She wondered which of his expressions she'd see in bed.

His change of demeanor and tone left her curious. She had a hard time believing the big, bad Scot would believe in such things. Would they believe in the truth if she'd told them? There was only one way to find out.

"I'm a medium." Quinn glanced between their confused faces and shrugged when they didn't respond. Guess not. Maybe she should have started with that and she would have been left to eat in peace.

"Explain," Ian demanded.

"You must have found your balls." He needed another dose in manners, but she silently chastised herself for taunting him. Her mother would be appalled and have a mini stroke from the way Quinn had been acting.

"Normally I donae tolerate a smart mouth on my wench," Ian exclaimed.

"Good thing I'm not your wench."

"I think she needs to be spanked into submission," Ian said.

Quinn's smile faded as she picked up her silverware and turned toward Ian. "Kinky, but if you think you're man enough, and willing to risk testing me to see what I can do with a knife, then bring it on." She raised her brow, daring him to make a move.

"Ian. Be nice." Collin's smooth baritone voice did little to stifle the anger stirring in her belly. Quinn wasn't normally the psychotic woman she was portraying. Not intentionally, although others might disagree. These men brought out the worst in her, specifically Ian.

"I apologize for Ian's lack of manners, Ms. Thatcher. He's just uptight about the curse, and we'd both like to know how you found out there was one, and how you found the emerald."

They wanted to know how she knew. Heck, if she were in their shoes, she'd be curious too. Quinn let out a long sigh and plopped another fry into her mouth before waving them in closer, into a huddle.

"I see dead people." She said it loud enough for the entire bar to hear, hoping that once these two were gone, no others would try to replace them.

"I knew she was crazy. The lass is a witch, and it explains her need to use violence."

"Surprisingly, you bring that out in me all by yourself. Now if you don't mind." Quinn gestured toward the door.

Neither one of them moved to stand. Ian's lips twisted at the corners, as if he enjoyed pushing her buttons. *What's wrong with me that I'm taking the bait? I'm smarter than that. I have more class in my pinky than the Neanderthal does in his biceps.* She rolled her eyes and ate another fry, debating if it was the lack of food making her so bitchy.

Collin leaned back and crossed his arms over his chest. "If you see dead people, prove it."

Quinn grabbed another fry and pointed it in his direction. "I'm not a performing monkey."

"Then why should we believe you? Maybe your family stole the stone."

Her family had been accused of worse. Her father was a shark in business; her mother was like the enforcer of her charity organization, and Quinn and her sisters... well they were psychic investigators that some skeptics referred to as Satan worshipers. She didn't know why she'd thought these guys would understand. She sounded crazy, and she was okay with that. Maybe she was going about this all wrong. Quinn let out an exaggerated sigh and gave Collin a tired glance.

"You have a chick in a blue dress that likes to hang out in one of your towers."

"Gwinnie." Ian lifted his beer toward Collin before he sipped.

"That's a legend, like the curse," Collin said, as if unconvinced.

Quinn didn't need to prove herself to these guys. What did they want from her?

"Obviously, you're a skeptic, and hey"—
she lifted her hands in surrender—"that's
your prerogative. I'm not here to change
your mind. I found your family heirloom
and returned it out of the goodness of my
heart. Can't you just let it go?"

Collin slipped a phone out of his
pocket. He scrolled in search of only God
knew what. It didn't matter. At least he
wasn't talking, and it was nice to know he
wasn't from the Stone Age, like the
electrical plugs in the small bed and
breakfast that called itself a hotel. A plug
adapter should be a requirement for
entering the country, much like a
passport.

"Do you know how much that emerald
is worth?" Ian asked.

"Nope, and I don't care." Quinn smiled
sweetly, shoving another fry in her mouth.
She wasn't about to let him bait her again.
Southern charm might be more effective. If
she acted nice, maybe they'd both get
bored and leave her to eat in peace.

Creases formed around Collin's eyes as
a smile split his lip. He abandoned his
phone and lifted the pint to his lips. The
fabric of his sleeve pulled deliciously
around his bulging biceps. *Focus.* He
wasn't a foreign booty call, and whatever
Mr. Tall, Dark, and Orgasmic wore under
his kilt would remain a mystery, although
judging by the bulge behind the zipper of

his jeans, she might be inclined to change her mind if he'd ask sweetly.

"Did you know there was a reward? Is that why you came?" Collin asked.

Clarence shimmered into the room behind both men, making the air colder. She spotted goosebumps rising on Collin's arms, yet everyone but her seemed oblivious to Clarence's presence. Quinn narrowed her eyes at the ghost that had sent her into this mess. No good deed went unpunished.

"I don't need your money, but I do know how you can repay me."

"There it is." McDougall lifted his pint in the air as if he'd won a prize. "I knew it. The lass is here for the money."

"If I'd wanted money, I would have kept the almost flawless seventy-five carat emerald. It was perfect minus the tiny cut mark, jackass. Think about what you just said."

"Ignore him, luv," Collin said, drawing her attention back to him. A glint of humor returned to his face. "The Menzies are indebted to you. How may I offer my services?"

His naked body in a warm bed with a can of Cool Whip and chocolate sauce for starters. Her undersexed body parts tingled in awareness at his Scottish lilt when he called her luv. "What can you tell me about the McNoltes?"

Clarence frowned and disappeared. Score one for her, finally.

"The gypsy witch—" Ian started to say when Collin held up his hand.

"Gypsy witch." Quinn's lips twisted into a big smile. "You guys believe in curses and gypsies, but not in psychics? How is that possible?"

"Aye." Collin picked up his phone again as she continued to eat her fries. "One foretold your arrival."

"You're kidding me, right?" Quinn tossed her fry onto the plate and asked with a smile.

Collin turned his phone around, making Quinn's lips part. She might as well have been looking in a mirror, minus the silk dress. "You did this, right? Someone snapped a picture of me while at your castle and you're a whiz at Photoshop or something?"

Collin's brows pitched as he exchanged a glance with Ian.

"You know... Photoshop? The photo editing software."

"I know of no such...software. This portrait is in the north tower and was painted by the gypsy who foretold your coming, and the return of the emerald."

And people thought she was weird. "That's great, guys, really." She rose and started loading up her napkin with uneaten fries. No way was she leaving them behind. "She must have been right. I came and returned your emerald. I hope your family paid her well. Now, if you don't mind, I've had a long day.

"What is this, national screw with the tourist day?" Quinn mumbled beneath her breath while grabbing her jacket and heading for the door.

"She said other things," Collin called out, stopping her in her tracks. Quinn slowly turned around to face them. The last of her energy drained as a headache started to form behind her eyes. "Did she tell you how to get rid of Clarence?"

He shook his head and rose. "No, nothing about a Clarence."

She lifted the greasy napkin holding her fries. "Right, well, have a nice life. I have to go check on my sick pilot to make sure we can leave in the morning. Cheerio." Or whatever. What did one say when parting ways in Scotland? No matter. She had no plans to use the word again. Nor need.

She saluted the bartender as she left, hoping that the gesture didn't mean anything derogatory. She'd made it outside when she felt Collin behind her.

"Your pilot is sick?" he asked as he walked beside her.

"Food poisoning or the flu. Not sure yet." Why had she bothered to answer?

Collin was like a stray dog. The more she encouraged him, the longer he'd stay.

"The town doc is a personal friend. Would you like me to call him and get your pilot looked at? Just to be safe."

"Uh..." Quinn glanced up at Collin. The hard lines of his face had softened. "Sure. That would be great." She'd checked in on Johnny to see if he could stomach anything to eat before going to the pub. He was huddled in blankets. With her luck, they'd be stranded in Scotland for an entire week. Would her father even send another plane in his fleet to pick them up? Probably not. "Why would you help us?"

"You returned the emerald, of course."

"Of course." Quinn smiled while trying to figure out his ulterior motive. Most men had one. He walked with her down the cobblestone street. The moonlight cast everything into shades of white and silver, leaving her pensive and on the lookout for Jack the Ripper. She should have packed her can of pepper spray or, at the very least, another pair of high heels. They turned the corner to the hotel and stopped in their tracks.

An ambulance and two police cars, with lights flashing, were parked in front of the hotel. The entrance was cordoned off with yellow crime scene tape draped from the one bush to the other, blocking the door. A police officer stood guard at the entrance. It was obvious this was the most excitement this sleepy town had seen in a long time. Nosy residents stood on the other side of the street draped in bathrobes over their nightclothes, silently watching and whispering to each other.

For the love of God...her pilot better not be dead. Collin placed his palm on Quinn's back and eased her toward the officer.

"Ted, what's going on?" Collin asked the young Barney Fife standing guard. He had acne covering his face.

"There's a guest with a potentially contagious disease. They believe he got some staff sick now too."

His voice was high pitched. The kid they trusted with a gun hadn't even hit puberty. Quinn's entire body stiffened as she registered his words while trying to peer around the officer. "Who's sick?" Her voice rose an octave as she tried to push closer to the door. "My pilot is in there. I have to go check on him."

Collin took her hand and eased her back to his side. His attempt to stifle her might have worked if he'd placed her hand on his crotch. Entwining their fingers wasn't enough to shut her up.

"Ted is it?" she asked. "Do you know who it is?"

"Aye, I think the maid who called it in said his name was Johnny Smith from the States. Is he your pilot?"

Quinn's stomach lurched and fell into her toes. Her legs felt weak, and she lost her voice, so she nodded while silently wondering if the sign on her forehead now read, *screw with this bitch.*

"What doctor is in there?" Collin asked, taking over the conversation.

"Pat Tanner, and he has locked the place down under quarantine until he has a diagnosis. He mentioned it was probably either measles or chickenpox."

"Quarantined. Excellent." Quinn slipped her fingers free and paced the small area, trying to figure out how to go about setting things right with Karma. Extra prayers, kindness, adopt those ten damn kittens? Crap. Her stomach recoiled, churning the greasy fries in her belly. Her throat tightened as concern ripped through her body.

Collin shook the man's hand. "Keep us posted and have Tanner call when he's done to give us an update. Could you also get word to Mr. Smith that I'm taking Ms. Thatcher to stay at the castle?"

"What? No." Quinn shook her head. "I can't leave him in there."

"Afraid you'll have to, Ms. Thatcher. I'll call when everything is clear."

Chapter 5

Collin led Quinn back toward the pub. His mind raced as he tried to understand how the disease had hit when the wee lass hadn't even been in Scotland for a full twenty-four hours. This was the only confirmation he needed. The curse was in full swing. Keeping her close while the rest played out was the only way he'd survive whatever happened next.

"I have to call Johnny's family," Quinn mumbled with her brows pinched together.

This was the first time he'd seen a panic-stricken expression on her face, and not the cool resolve she'd previously portrayed. She was truly concerned, and she wasn't even aware the worst was yet to come. "You should wait until we hear back from the doctor. There's no need to get them worried until we have some facts."

Quinn nodded and stayed surprisingly quiet as he helped her into the passenger side of his truck. Ian was wise to wait until she was inside the truck before he approached. "Judging by the look on the lassie's face, I'm guessing the curse has started."

"Aye. The hotel is quarantined."

"Disease was the first item listed in the curse." Ian patted Collin's back as he rounded the truck. "If it follows suit, next up is death. You might want to lock your chamber doors. Good luck, ole friend."

Collin nodded as an unshakable feeling came over him that they'd all need a bit of luck to come out unscathed. The drive to the castle was uneventful, and yet he knew what was waiting inside. He'd be lucky if all of the staff didn't up and quit when they found out he'd brought the American home with him for more than a midnight tryst.

"You know this isn't necessary." Quinn finally spoke as Collin killed the ignition in the driveway. "If there is another hotel in town, I can stay there."

"Donae be ridiculous. You returned the emerald. You'll be my guest." He gave her a reassuring smile as they both got out of the truck on the rock-covered driveway. The crunch of rocks beneath Collin's boots was the only sound in the eerie night. Even the breeze from earlier was gone, as if warning him of things to come. "Besides, there isnae another hotel in town."

"I can't imagine why you aren't overflowing with tourists. I'm sure it has nothing to do with Mr. Grabby Hands, or the ancient hotel, or even the lack of food choices."

Collin chuckled. The drive to the castle had restored her spirit and smart replies. He was much more capable of dealing with a feisty lass than a scared one.

"Give Scotland a chance. It will grow on you."

"Like fungus beneath toenails," she mumbled as he led her into the castle.

The normally loud atmosphere had been replaced with stillness. The only sound that greeted them was the ticking of the tall grandfather clock. The staff had already left for the evening, and those who lived in the castle were tucked away in their rooms. Quinn slowed her step and frowned.

"This isn't what I expected."

"What did you expect?" Collin rubbed his neck while trying to view the space with fresh eyes. The renovations over the years had made the castle more welcoming and less primitive. The cream-colored walls complemented the expensive marble floors. The decorations and furniture were antique but tastefully placed around the room. A vase with roses sat in the middle of an antique table of the large open entryway. Most women walked over and sniffed the fragrance. Quinn Thatcher wasn't most women. She eyed it with a bit of alarm.

"This is modern-day chic. I pictured primitive and manly. Maybe a wall filled with pictures of past lairds and full suits of armor with shields and swords. Half-clad maids with boobs hanging out while perched on the knees of drunken men."

"You've confused my castle with Ian's. We donae have the drunken men or half-dressed lassies, but we do have the armor and shields. We keep those in the ballroom."

"Right, ballroom. I'm sure you use that all the time."

"You'd be surprised." Collin risked life and limb by placing his hand on the small of her back and leading her toward the stairs. The soft flannel of her shirt kept him from feeling the heat from her body. She either didn't notice that he was touching her or was too tired to protest. His bet was on the latter. "Let's get you settled in the guest room while I check in with the doctor at the hotel."

Collin led her to the room next to his. It was the second best room in the castle, and reserved for the lady of the house. It was prim, proper, and elegant, nothing like the outspoken, spunky American who would be staying in the space. Regardless, she deserved the best for what she'd returned to his family.

He pushed the door open and had expected her to love the space. To actually praise the beauty of the space, like most overnight guests would. He should have known Quinn wasn't like an ordinary visitor.

Quinn covered her nose sneezing continuously as she vehemently shook her head and pressed her back against the hallway wall.

"Is it no' to your liking?" Collin asked, unsure of her problem.

"You're trying to kill me, aren't you? I would have expected it from Ian, but not you."

"All of the rooms in the castle have been renovated. What's the problem with this room?"

She pointed an accusing finger at the room. "I'm highly allergic to the flowers, and that room is covered in them."

She grasped her throat as if it was difficult to breathe, so Collin quickly shut the door. "I'm sorry. I dinnae know."

The hand at her throat moved to cover her heart. "Do you have any other spare rooms that aren't overflowing with those killers?"

Collin stifled his smile. That was the first time anyone had ever referred to beautiful flowers as killers.

"Aye, there is only one room in the castle without the killers."

"Good, I'll take it."

Collin pushed open his bedroom door and gestured for her to enter.

She walked inside. Her eyes scanned the entire room before walking over to the bed and picking up Collin's kilt, which he'd discarded earlier. "Is this your way of trying to get me into your bed?"

Collin locked eyes with hers and slid the kilt from her fingers, slightly grazing her knuckles with his touch. Her emerald eyes lightened to the shade of grass covered with morning dew. Her red, plump lips lifted in a smile. He was finding Quinn was unabashed. Where most women would have blushed from the touch or his proximity, Quinn looked as though she reveled in the playfulness.

Clearing his throat, Collin grabbed the shirt he'd worn earlier from the bed and stepped back out of her personal space. "Nay, when you sleep with me, it willnae be because there was no other place for you to rest your head. I'll sleep with the killers until I can have them all removed in the morning."

"When and if I take you to bed, I can guarantee sleep won't be on the agenda." She winked, gave him a full grin, and pressed her heated palm against his chest, pushing him backward toward the door. "Good night, Laird Menzie."

"Collin," he corrected.

"Good night, Collin." She stood on her tiptoes and pressed her soft lips to his cheek before flicking the door closed in his face. His heartbeat quickened, and his pants grew tight, while he wondered what those lips would feel like elsewhere on his body.

Collin stood in the hallway, momentarily stunned, when the door suddenly flew open. Quinn cupped his cheeks and pressed her lips to his in a full-out assault. He'd barely had time to drop the items he'd been holding to free his hands when she broke the kiss and stepped back.

"Sorry, I couldn't resist. Maybe next time you can play dress up and wear the skirt." She grinned again and shut the door.

"Only if I get to pick out your dress, wench," Collin called out and grabbed the clothes off the floor. Her laughter rang out as he tossed the clothes onto the bed in the middle of the killing fields. He was playing with fire. The thought made him pause. Fire was in the curse. Could it have been referring to the sparks of chemistry that they shared, or were heated flames really a possibility?

Collin jogged down the stairs and into his office to find Ramsey waiting inside with a file in his hands.

"I wasnae expecting you," Collin said, heading to the crystal decanter across the room. He poured himself a double shot of whiskey and threw back the shot, welcoming the fire in his throat.

"How long have I been your financial advisor?"

"Five years, but we both know you're more than my advisor. If it wasnae for you, I'd still be dealing with the castle reconstruction from the fire and having to contend with the architects and insurance people." Collin answered without hesitation. He'd trusted Ramsey with his entire portfolio after a stock market tip that had quadrupled the worth. Not to mention the headache he saved from having to figure out the castle blueprints.

"I'm surprised you dinnae call me," Ramsey said and sat in one of the chairs opposite Collin's desk. "I hear your family emerald was returned by a redheaded American who resembles the lady in the portrait."

"You heard correctly. I put the emerald in the safe, and Quinn will be staying here until her sick pilot has recovered."

Ramsey gave a slow nod and tossed the file in his hands onto the desk. "Yes, I heard her name was Quinn Thatcher. Did she tell you she's a medium?"

"She told the whole bar." Collin chuckled, remembering the way she unceremoniously announced her profession as if she'd be viewed as a leper. If she'd thought her words would make them leave, she'd been wrong. Collin was nothing if not more intrigued. He picked up the file. "What's this?"

"I did a background check on your guest. It isnae every day that a mysterious woman shows up at your door to return something so valuable. Have you figured out her angle?"

"She disnae have one. She's stuck here by circumstance." Collin's smile fell as he flipped the folder open and read the report inside.

Quinn Thatcher, single, age 35. Ms. Thatcher is a co-owner of Linked Inc., a multimillion-dollar company well known as a psychic hotline and detective agency in the States. It went on to state that she worked with numerous law enforcement agencies to help find missing people and solve homicides.

"This proves she disnae have any ulterior motive. She hasnae asked for a reward or money, and she'd actually planned to leave in the morning, until her pilot got sick."

Collin closed the file.

"Flip to the last page." Ramsey nodded toward the file.

Collin did as he asked. He scanned the computer printed article's headline: *Psychic unable to predict the untimely and questionable death of fiancé who left her with a fortune.*

"This disnae prove she had anything to do with his death."

"It disnae prove she dinnae," Ramsey said, rising. "As the chief financial advisor of your estate, and foremost, as your friend, I thought you should know who's staying under your roof."

Collin knew exactly who was sleeping in his bed. Quinn was a mystery to him in most ways, but there was no denying that she was the center of the curse, or that she was the first woman in a long time who reminded him that he was more than a laird. He was simply a man who had needs, wants, and desires. Exploring their chemistry was worth the price of keeping her around. Curse or no curse.

Chapter 6

Quinn woke to find dust motes dancing in the sunshine streaming in through the window. Her big lumberjack boots were gone, and the covers lay over her chest, the silky texture at odds with the large man who usually occupied the bed.

She pulled the covers over her eyes and groaned. The Highlander's musky scent filled her nose. The trip hadn't been a dream. She flung the covers off her body and stared up at the stone ceiling. "This is payback for everything I've ever done wrong in my life, isn't it?"

"No, dear, it's destiny." She heard the unmistakable ghostly whisper as the temperature dropped, chilling her cheeks.

She sat up to find not one but three ghosts staring back at her from the foot of the bed. The sight of them would have sent normal people screaming and running from the room, but she'd never been confused with normal. The man in the middle had a full red beard and matching hair color. A scar covered his left cheek and dipped down his neck, disappearing into green checkered plaid. His eyes were the same baby blue that matched Collin's.

The woman in the royal blue dress, from the north tower, stood next to him. Her hand clutched where her heart would be. Her brunette curls were secured with a ruby-accented comb.

The ghost on Redbeard's left didn't resemble Collin at all. His hair was white and wavy, but there was no mistaking the colors of his tartan. She'd seen the exact same pattern yesterday on McGrabs-a-lot. He was related to Ian without question.

"Funny how you're not haters because of the color of your plaid in the afterlife. Care to tell me how to get out of your motherland?"

"I told you she can see us," the woman announced.

"Gwinnie, isn't it?" Quinn said, sliding off the bed. "I don't suppose you can explain to Collin, your great-great-whatever, that there isn't a curse?"

They glanced between one another before turning their stares back to Quinn.

"You will set things right," Gwinnie announced before all three of them shimmered out of sight.

"I'll take that as a no," Quinn grumbled, not even trying to cover the irritation lacing her voice. She spotted her boots by the door and slipped them on. After running her fingers through her hair, she used the rubber band on her wrist to pull it up in a ponytail. If she'd had her way, the doctor and police would give her access to her room and clear Johnny and her to return home.

Quinn stepped into the hall to hunt down Collin. The sickly sweet smell of last night was gone. Intrigued, she peered into the bedroom next door. Not a single petal or leaf was in sight.

"He kept his word." Warmth that she hadn't felt in five years flooded her chest. She shoved the feeling away. He was just a man trying to accommodate her because she'd returned his gem. Still, the gesture was sweet. Quinn went out on the landing and stared below. Maids were dusting the room. The vase that had been sitting on the antique table was gone, and a smile split her lips.

Jogging down the stairs, she smiled politely at the maid who'd pinched her yesterday. "Can you tell me where to find Collin?"

"Aye, Miss Thatcher."

"My friends call me Quinn, and since we're already on a pinching basis, I guess that includes you."

"Your friends pinch you?" she asked, her brows dipped in confusion.

"That and worse."

"I'm Abigail, miss. If you'll just follow me, the others are sitting down to morning breakfast."

"Thanks, Abby."

Quinn walked alongside her as she made several turns down different hallways. They passed by another large entrance where Quinn slowed to get a better look. Old-timey paintings hung on the wall, along with a crest and crossed swords. Suits of armor did indeed line the wall, making her chuckle. "Must be the ballroom."

"Yes, miss."

"Quinn," she reminded her.

"Yes, Miss Quinn."

"Just Quinn."

"Quinn," she repeated. "I'll be happy to help you if you need anything during your stay. The staff has been informed of your presence, and we are at your service."

"I don't suppose you know how to fly a plane."

"No, Miss...Quinn, afraid no'."

Abby stopped at the entrance to the dining room and gestured. Quinn gave her a good old southern smile and stepped inside the room, expecting to find Collin sitting alone at the table. She was wrong.

Chairs scratched the floor as three men stood. A blonde-haired woman sitting next to Collin at the table ignored Quinn's arrival and continued drinking from the fine china. Quinn had learned early in life to ignore the aura's around everyone's body, but this woman's color was hard to ignore. It was the same color as baby poop

Good thing the food didn't smell the same way. The smell of fresh bacon drifted to her nose, making her stomach growl.

"Quinn, please come in and join us for breakfast."

"If I can just get a lift back into town, I can grab something from the pub." Quinn gestured with her thumb over her shoulder as she silently wondered if Abby knew how to drive.

"Great idea. I can take her." The woman at the table shoved back her chair and raised her brow with a forced smile. Quinn had seen that smile before. She'd given it a time or two. It oozed "woman on her period ready to fight to the death for the last piece of chocolate in the universe." Game on, sister. Quinn gave her a lopsided grin and sauntered into the room straight up to Collin, ignoring the others. She rested her hand on his bulging bicep and met his gaze. "Thanks for letting me sleep in your room last night. It was magical."

Ian busted out in laughter as the woman's eyes narrowed in contempt. The other man at the table rested his palm on Blondie's arm as if ready to stop her from scratching out Quinn's eyes. Quinn wasn't worried. There was plenty of silverware within reach.

Collin's eyes sparkled as he smiled down at Quinn and cupped her cheek. His palm was warm and soft to the touch as he lowered his head, never dropping her gaze until his lips were mere inches from hers. "You thought last night was magical? You havenae seen anything yet."

He slipped his arm around Quinn's waist and pulled her flush against his hard body as he kissed her lips. She didn't question why he was helping her bait the blonde woman; she didn't care. The heat of his mouth seared Quinn to the soul as her heart raced frantically in her chest. His tongue toyed with hers, sipping, taking, and meeting hers at every move. Touché.

He slowly pulled away. "You'll stay and eat, then I'll show you the grounds."

"You win." She grinned, already spying the biscuits on the table. She'd planned to grab one on her way out, but this was so much more fun than eating alone. She silently wondered how many locals she could piss off before Johnny got well.

"Ian, you wouldn't mind moving down to make room for Quinn, would you?"

"Of course not. I've finished anyway." Ian moved his plate and put a fresh one in its place before holding out Quinn's chair.

Blondie snapped her mouth shut and tossed her napkin on her uneaten food.

"Well." She huffed. "I've lost my appetite. If you'll excuse me." She stomped from the room.

"It was a pleasure meeting you," Quinn called out after her, hoping for one last jab, even though she really wanted to sing, *Booyah, I got your boyfriend,* and then do a chair dance that would make her mother cringe. Okay, so maybe that was a dick move, or what men would refer to as a cock block, but she didn't like Blondie's sneer or her puke-green aura.

The other guy, who had been at the table, excused himself seconds after the woman, and Ian grabbed a biscuit and raised it in a wave. "It's always a pleasure, Quinn."

"Aww shucks, there's no reason to lie to my face, Ian."

Ian chuckled as he continued out of the room, leaving Collin and Quinn alone.

"I thought the blonde Barbie was going to jump me," Quinn said, grabbing a biscuit and muffin from the table. She plopped down in Ian's old seat.

"She's jealous," Collin said, retaking his seat. "She's been trying to get me to kiss her like that since she stepped foot inside the castle. I'm going to owe you for the rest of my life, first returning my emerald and now getting Margarete to leave me alone. Avoiding her was a full-time job. I'm beginning to think you're my good luck charm."

"Now, Collin, I'm sure if you had just told her you only like brunettes or redheads with big breasts, she would have taken the hint."

"I'm afraid you're wrong. I dinnae think anything would have ever stopped her from trying. She would have dyed her hair and scheduled a breast implant."

"If you don't like her, then why is she here?" she asked before sinking her teeth into the blueberry muffin. She moaned in appreciation. The muffin was fluffy and flavorful, definitely not from a package of ingredients that she couldn't pronounce. "I'm going to make your cook my new best friend."

"She'll be happy to hear that. You have a healthy appetite." Collin grinned.

"Doesn't everyone?" Quinn asked before taking another bite.

"Margarete eats like a bird and complains about the food much of the time."

"Tell me again why you tolerate her."

"She's an interior decorator, restoring the rooms on the west side of the castle back to their former glory after an unfortunate fire."

Quinn swallowed. "Ah, you need her but don't want a booty call. I get it. It's like that time my pool guy took off his shirt. Tempting, but he must have been drinking the pool chemicals because he was short a few screws. Well, not screws if you know what I mean." Quinn wiggled her brows. "I'm sure he got plenty of action, just not from me. Speaking of screwing, is the universe still playing with me, or did my pilot make a miraculous recovery?"

"I spoke with the doctor last night before I tucked you in. Johnny is still very sick, and the official diagnosis is measles. Since a rash has appeared, he is contagious."

"How long am I looking at?"

"Possibly two weeks, could be less. They've transported him to a hospital in the nearby town. One other housekeeper had a fever and was taken as a precaution."

Quinn's heart fell into her stomach. Her annoyance was replaced with concern. Poor, poor Johnny. Here she was sitting in a castle with amazing food, having fun pissing off the locals, and Johnny was stuck in a hospital, probably covered in anti-itch lotion. Quinn's skin crawled. She pulled her shirt away from her chest and peered down at her creamy skin. She sighed in relief. False alarm. No rashes.

"Your ghosts are conspiring against me," she announced, pouring a cup of coffee from the carafe. "I woke up to find three of them staring at me. Gwinnie thinks I'm here to set things right."

"Who were the other two?" Collin asked, before sipping his coffee.

"Well, we didn't have a formal introduction, but one looks like an older version of you with red hair and beard, and the other was a white-haired fellow wearing Ian's colors."

"Sounds like Alastair, my four times great-grandfather, and his rival, Alexander McDougall. The stone was stolen during their time."

"Well, now it's returned. I've set things right; so why are they being creepy and watching me sleep?"

"The curse," he answered as though he believed it himself. Quinn was starting to get the suspicion that he did. Who was the weird one now?

"I don't believe in curses," she announced. She didn't even want to know what the curse entailed. No ancestor or dead gypsy had any say in her life or her future.

"You've made that abundantly clear, but arenae you the least bit interested?"

"I'm about as interested as a toll booth operator, on a road closed for construction, looking for the next car." She shook her head. The thought of being the catalyst of the curse gave her a headache.

"Disease, death, fire, and fallen men are foretold in the tale. Measles is just the start."

"Hey." She pulled at the blueberry muffin. "I wasn't the one to inflict the measles. It's just a coincidence that my pilot was the carrier. Did your curse mention that?"

"Actually, it reads: A woman with hair of fire, and eyes the color of the stolen stone, will descend from the sky. Her word will carry a bite and sting worse than the fiercest beast, making the lines between past and present blur."

"Any redhead with green eyes fits that description."

"Disease will spread; death will follow; walls will crumble, and men will fall."

"That's a lot to put on my shoulders, don't you think?" Quinn sipped her coffee.

"Friend or foe, it is she who controls the Menzie destiny and will bring down the deceit of once noble men, making them fall from grace into hell."

"Don't you think that's a bit vague?" she asked. "That's like saying one of your unborn children will be a girl. Why not give details and say one of your children will be a unicorn with rainbow hair? Now that would be interesting, and something I'd stick around to watch."

Collin smiled. "You arenae quite right, Quinn Thatcher."

"Words to live by," she said, standing and slipping her phone with the half-dead battery from her pocket. "I need to call Johnny's family and check in with my sisters."

"Reception is best outside, if you're going to use your cell phone."

"Thanks." She picked up her uneaten biscuit and headed for the door, only pausing before she stepped out of the room. She turned back to face him. "I promise not to bring down any of your walls."

"Donae promise what you cannae control, Quinn."

"See, that's the thing." Her face brightened as she smiled. "Tearing down walls requires effort and will. I have neither, so I think your castle and you are safe."

"Only time will tell."

Chapter 7

Collin watched Quinn through the kitchen window as he passed along Quinn's compliments on the cooking. Mavis' husband, Angus, stood beside Collin, watching as Quinn held her phone up to the sky, as if looking for the best reception.

"You dinnae tell her it was best near the cliffs?" Angus asked.

"Nay." Collin inwardly smiled. "It's best to keep an eye on her the entire time she's here, and I cannae see her if she goes over there."

"This woman is wise, no' to mention fierce, bringing Ian to his knees. She'll figure out the best place for reception and the curse." Mavis chuckled, wiping her flour-covered hands on her apron. "Did you ask her what Ramsey found?"

"How do you know what Ramsey found?" Collin asked, turning to face the white-haired woman who'd practically raised him.

"Nothing can get by that woman. She knows all." Angus nudged his arm.

"Well, have you asked her about it?" Mavis asked, not answering where she heard the rumor.

"Nay," Collin answered, turning back to find Quinn was walking out of sight toward the corner of the castle, in the exact direction of the cliffs. Damn woman.

"It's probably wise you leave the wounded animal alone. We all have a past, and she's apparently lost someone she loved. If she thinks you're attacking her, you'll likely find that her bite is worse than her bark. No reason to anger the lassie if you donae have to. I hear she's already causing a stir with Margarete."

"Aye, that she has." Collin inwardly smiled, not wanting to let on that he whole-heartedly approved of Quinn's method.

"Probably for the best you keep Ms. Thatcher close and warn her about

Margarete. There's nothing like a woman scorned on the verge of losin' the trophy she's been eyeing."

"I think Quinn can take her."

"I'd lay odds on your American." Angus nudged Collin's arm again. "She's a fine lass, indeed."

"That she is," Collin answered, heading out the back door to hunt for Quinn.

He rounded the edge of the castle's stone walls, expecting to find Quinn standing at the cliff's edge with the phone pressed against her ear. The rocky cliffs were empty, not a soul in sight.

"Quinn," he yelled out. His gaze searched the nearby forest as he moved closer.

"Help."

He heard the faint cry over the sound of waves crashing against the rocks.

"Quinn. Where are you, lass?" he yelled louder. His heart pounded against his ribs as unease coursed through his veins. His boots pounded against the packed dirt as he ran toward the rocky ledge.

"I'm down here," she called out.

He skidded to a stop, knocking a rock over the edge. The rock smacked her in the middle of the forehead as her fingers clung to one of the smooth boulders. Her body dangled over the edge.

"I thought you said that I'd make men fall, not that *I* would be the one falling."

Collin lay down on his stomach and held out both hands. "I'm going to pull you up. Give me your hand, Quinn."

She shook her head. "If I let go, I'll fall."

Her fingertips were turning as white as her cheeks. "I'm coming down."

Hopping up from his position, he moved to sit on his rear and then eased down the rocky ledge until his foot found purchase on one of the larger boulders below. Wrapping his fingers around her arm for a firm grip, he lifted her and pulled her toward him until he had her tightly in his arms, refusing to let her go. Her racing heart pounded against his chest as she looked up into his eyes. Color started to return to her cheeks as he held her close.

"Thanks for saving me."

"You donae strike me as someone who needs saving, lass."

Glancing over her shoulder to the sharp rocks below, she trembled in his hold. "I'm normally not. I think Scotland might be bad for my health."

"Let's get you back on stable ground and you can tell me what happened." Collin lifted her light body at the waist and hoisted her toward the ledge. Placing his hands on her gorgeous jean-covered ass, he eased her over the ledge before hoisting himself back up.

Quinn was lying with her arms and legs spread wide on the grassy knoll. Her chest rose and fell as she stared up at the forming clouds above. "I thought I was a goner."

Collin sat down next to her. "No' on my watch. You want to tell me how you ended up down there?"

"I must have slipped," Quinn said, worrying her lip between her teeth. He could tell she was holding something back. She rolled toward him. "When you came out, you dinnae see anyone around, did you?"

"Nay."

"That's what I thought," she said, getting to her feet. She peered over the edge. "That brings all new meaning to the phrase dead phone."

Collin got to his feet and glanced over the edge. Her phone lay in pieces on another rocky ledge about ten feet down. "You can use the phone in my office to make your calls."

"Thanks." She patted his chest. "I guess that makes us even on one account."

"What's that?"

"I saved your life from Margarete's advances, and a possible loveless marriage to a woman who would never truly appreciate you, and in return you saved mine."

She gave a saucy wink and started back toward the castle. Was everything a joke to this woman? She'd almost died, and yet she was...optimistic. Most women would have been crying in his arms. Not Quinn, he was learning...Never Quinn.

Collin glanced back once more to the busted phone. If he hadn't followed her, she'd potentially be dead on the rock. Maybe the curse had been wrong. He'd turned to leave when he saw something sparkling on the ground beneath the leaves. He squatted and moved the leaves and dirt away. A broach was poking out of the ground. Running the pad of his thumb over the stone revealed a ruby beneath the grime. He'd seen this piece before but couldn't for the life of him remember where. How it had managed to be in that spot was yet another puzzle in a string of mysteries to solve.

Chapter 8

Quinn was led into Collin's office to make her calls. Leaning back against the wood doors, she rested her scraped hands against her knees, trying to slow her racing heart as blood pounded in her temples. Her annoyance spiraled when she noticed her hands and arms shaking. Her fall hadn't been an accident like she'd let Collin believe. She hadn't slipped or lost her balance. That had been a real hand pressed against her back, giving her a tiny shove in hopes of giving her an untimely demise. Someone with a heartbeat and body had tried to push her over the edge. Anger stirred in her belly with renewed fire. She clenched her jaw as her chest tightened. They didn't know who they were dealing with, but with a little help, they'd soon find out.

She rounded the desk and sat in Collin's worn leather chair. It was cool to the touch and smelled of mink oil and saddle soap, like the one in her father's study. The furniture in Collin's office matched the rest of the house, solid with class and a little hint of manly added to the mix. Quinn picked up the phone and dialed. Her sister, Cara, answered on the first ring.

"How's Scotland?"

"It's trying to kill me," Quinn answered.

"The country?"

"Yeah, but never mind that. Johnny has the measles, so we're stuck here for a while. Can you let everyone know that we're going to be delayed?

"It's the curse, isn't it? Did you get rid of the emerald?"

"Within minutes of arriving, but apparently the Menzies commissioned a gypsy to paint some portraits about how the curse would play out, and you won't believe it, but one of the portraits depict someone who looks like me. Now everyone is in an uproar." Seeing the picture on the phone left Quinn bewildered, if not a bit intrigued, not that she'd tell her sister. Cara would personally fly over to drag

Quinn back kicking and screaming to reality. Well, at least she'd try.

"I told you not to go. I warned you that thing is cursed. You need to come home."

"Not yet."

Cara let out a loud, long sigh. "So how is Scotland trying to kill you?"

"Oh, you know." Quinn waved her hand as if Cara could see her and began tapping her foot. "The flowers are on steroids and are everywhere. There's a pissed-off woman who thinks I'm out to steal her man. Oh, and there was an incident where someone tried to push me off a cliff."

"What!" Cara's squeal made Quinn's momentarily deaf and caused her ears ring. "Get on the next plane and get out of there. Now," Cara demanded as any good sister might. Quinn gave her props for trying, even if she'd ignore Cara's demands. She couldn't order Quinn around in person, so why did she think she'd accomplish it from another country?

"When have you ever known me to run from a fight?" Quinn's nervously jumping leg stopped mid-bounce.

"This isn't a joke." Cara's voice lowered to a scolding boil.

"I'll be fine. I can't leave the hunky Scot to fend for himself. He's not equipped. Not until I figure out what's going on."

83

"Quinn Elizabeth."

"That doesn't even work when Mom is mad." Quinn chuckled. "Collin needs a savior, so I'm going to give him one."

"Quinn, be reasonable. You don't know what you're up against, and you don't know those people. They could all be psycho crazy killers. Come home."

"I can't. Not even if I wanted to, but you're right. I might not know what I'm up against, but I do know three ghosts that can give me all the juicy details. Gotta go, sis, love you, and if I die, you get my shoe collection and you can say you were right."

"Quinnnnnnn,"

Cara meant well, but was it bad that all Quinn heard was blah, blah, blah? Cara was blood. She should know better than most that Quinn would do things her way. Changing her mind wasn't easily achieved. She'd been talked into it once and her ex fiancé had paid the ultimate price and lost his life. Never again. Danny was a prime example of what happened when her gut instincts weren't heeded. His handsome face flashed before her eyes, making her heart clench and her stomach roll. It was hard to believe that five years had passed since that fateful night when he'd turned her life upside down. She'd survived losing him; she'd damn sure survive Scotland.

Quinn left the office, stopping Abby in the hall. "Do you drive?"

"No, miss, but Angus does, and he's in the kitchen?"

Quinn wasn't stranded and at anyone's mercy. Hallefreakinlujah. There was a God, and at the moment, he was on her side. "Thank you." Quinn all but sang the words.

"Would you like me to show you the way?" she asked.

"Nope, I'll find it but thanks for your help."

Ten minutes later, after multiple wrong turns and questionable looks, Quinn followed the delicious smell of fresh-baked bread until she finally found the kitchen.

Angus had a woman wrapped in his arms, engaging in a sensuous lip lock with both hands squeezing her backside. Quinn would have been embarrassed, but she was too stunned that the old coot was getting some action.

"That better be Mrs. Angus, or I'm telling your wife to double your chores."

The couple pulled apart. The white-haired woman's cheeks were as pink as the stew meat on the counter ready to be tossed into the pot. She smoothed her hair with one hand and playfully tapped Angus on the arm with the other. Thank God Quinn had gotten there when she had. She'd need to bleach her eyes if she'd caught them getting busy on the counter. Some things just couldn't be unseen.

"Aye. You must be Quinn Thatcher, my new best friend. I'm Mavis, the keeper of Angus' chore list."

A giddiness claimed Quinn, and her grin grew. This woman was the creator of the amazing muffins. No wonder Angus was getting frisky. "Your muffins have ruined me from enjoying the processed foods back home, but no matter. I have every intention of sneaking you back into the States." Quinn knocked Angus on the arm. "You can come too."

"I like you, Quinn Thatcher," Mavis said, picking up a plate of cookies. She held it out to Quinn. "I baked you some American cookies to make you feel more at home."

"Mavis, dear, she just had breakfast," Angus said as he moved to take the plate.

"You've got to be quicker than that, old man," Quinn said, snatching the entire plate out of his reach. She coveted the chocolate chip cookies as if they were the oxygen she needed to survive. She took a bite into the warm cookie. The melted chocolate coated her tongue. Her eyes closed in bliss, and she might have moaned. She'd never tasted anything so divine. "It's dangerous to stand between a woman and dessert."

"I'll have to remember that," Collin said as he entered the kitchen. He took a cookie from the plate and inhaled his in two bites. He went to take another one and Mavis grabbed the plate. "You'll ruin your lunch."

"He will, but I won't," Quinn said while slipping another one from the plate. A spatula came down against the top of her hand, but no amount of pain from the cookie warden could have made her drop that cookie. "I don't suppose you know how to make pizza, do you?"

Mavis' eyes twinkled as though she held all kinds of culinary knowledge over mere mortals. She probably did.

"I hear you need a ride," Collin asked.

"Oh yeah." Quinn had gone momentarily brain dead, first with Angus' kissing escapades, and then because of savoring the melting chocolate chips. She'd had her fair share of cookies and chocolate but nothing as orgasmic as Mavis' treats. It was official; Quinn was taking Mavis home with her if she had to beg, borrow, or steal. It didn't take much to make her happy. "The voyeurism and food made me forget. Had I known Mavis was such a great cook, I would have bartered her for the emerald."

"I wouldnae have traded, but I'd consider time share." Collin laughed, and Quinn broke the cookie in half and held it up to his lips, rewarding him like a child willing to share his toys.

"Mmmm." He mumbled as he chewed. "Where'd you need to go?"

"Into town to grab my bags and buy some more clothes. I hadn't expected to stay an entire week or more."

"I'll grab my keys," Angus said, gesturing over his shoulder.

"Nay, I'll drive Quinn. You can supervise the staff as they start setting up the ballroom for this weekend. Make sure they donae try to sword fight like they did last year."

"Ohhh, a party. Will you wear your skirt?" Quinn teased, following Collin out of the kitchen.

"Aye, I'll be wearing my kilt. It's an annual tradition to keep the peace between the Menzies and McDougalls. Where the singles mingle in search of finding true love in the other's clan."

"Seriously?" Quinn asked, following him out of the castle to the truck parked out front. "Do you parade the women like a herd of cattle, or do you chaps prefer wet T-shirt contests?"

"Nay." Collin chuckled, opening the truck door. He stopped her before she got in. Using the pad of his thumb, he swiped at the corner of her mouth. "You've got something right there."

Heat swirled in his eyes as his body pressed against hers, making her stomach flutter in delight and her breath hitch from his touch.

"I was saving that for later." Quinn slipped past him and wiped at the corners of her mouth. He was good. She could see how any woman might fall under his spell. She shoved the thoughts aside and cleared her throat. Her objective didn't include taking the man to bed but saving Collin and herself from whoever had tried to turn her into fish food. Although... there wasn't a reason why she couldn't do both.

Quinn waited until Collin pulled out of the castle driveway before blurting out, "Who has the most to gain if the curse plays out?"

Collin was quiet, as if mulling it over. "Ian," he finally answered. "The last portrait depicts someone handing him the emerald."

"Are you sure it's him in the picture?"

"Aye. He has a matching birthmark on his wrist."

"And who has the most to lose?" Quinn asked, trying to remember some of the words from the curse. Each time she tried, the word death kept flashing in her mind.

"I'm no' sure. Neither the gypsy nor the curse gave names. We have only the portraits and the poem. It said that you'd bring a once noble man to ruin."

"Let's not forget the part of the poem that mentions fire and death to contend with," she reminded him.

"Do you trust all of your staff and the people close to you?"

"Aye. I trust them all." Collin's words were strained as he pumped the brakes. The truck was picking up speed going down the hill. "The brakes are no' working."

Quinn's whole body stiffened. At the bottom of the hill was a sharp curve, and if he didn't make the turn, they'd both turn into ghosts. She wasn't about to live an eternity in this foreign land.

She reached for the door latch as her heart raced faster with each passing second.

"You cannae jump."

"Wanna bet? We both are, on the count of three. One, two..." She didn't wait until three before shoving the door open. Her body tensed at the sight of the gravel road beneath the tires. The grass was about a foot away. "Three," she yelled at the same time Collin's door opened. She launched away from the road and landed in the hard packed grass and leaves and continued to roll before coming to a stop. She sat up, rubbing her head and trying to refocus her eyes. Her gaze landed on

Collin on the other side of the road before their gazes flew to the truck and they both watched in horror as it disappeared over the cliff and out of sight. The sound of crunching metal and burst of shooting flames filled the quiet afternoon. Quinn lay back in the grass, afraid to move and taking inventory of all of her body parts. Her back ached, but that was nothing compared to the invisible sledgehammer pounding against her head. The jump could have been worse. The side of the road could have been covered in heather. Quinn's vision blurred and her head started to sway. She closed her eyes to fight the fainting feeling and lost her battle as a dark void consumed her consciousness.

Chapter 9

Collin's entire body ached, but that didn't compare to the relief he felt in his heart when he met Quinn's gaze. They both watched in horror as his truck disappeared from sight. The relief in his body was short-lived when he noticed Quinn collapsing back to the ground. Was she hurt?

He ignored his bruises and pushed through his protesting muscles, getting up to stagger across the road. Quinn lay unmoving. Only the rise and fall of her chest calmed his racing heart. Collin ran his hands over her arms and legs. Scrapes and bruises covered some of her porcelain skin, but nothing appeared to be broken.

"Quinn, luv." Collin rested his palm on her cheek.

Her eyes fluttered open to meet his gaze. "Did your curse happen to mention cut brakes?"

"No mention of cut brakes, just disease, death, fire, and ruin."

"If we hadn't gotten out, that one ride could have taken care of all of it." Her gaze lifted to something behind him before she narrowed her eyes. "Clarence, if you weren't already dead, I'd kill you again."

"Clarence, the ghost from the States that you're trying to get rid of?" Collin asked, glancing over his shoulder to find the field and road empty. "I think you hit your head a bit harder than I thought. There's no one here but us." He turned back and felt the back of her head for any sign that he was right.

"He's standing right behind you," Quinn said, brushing his hands from her body. She tried to shove Collin away, yet he remained unmoving, unsure if she was really unhurt or just annoyed.

"Ask him if he knows who cut the brakes," Collin suggested while helping her stand. He lowered his gaze down her backside, making sure he hadn't missed any injuries.

"Whose ass do I need to kick?" Quinn asked, resting her balled fist on her hip. Not even a second later, she tossed her hands into the air and yelled, "Oh, now you're not talking. What happened to the karaoke, asshole?"

Her red cheeks glistened in the afternoon sun as he picked leaves out of her hair, fighting his urge to run his fingers through her soft tendrils. "It looks like we're walking."

"It's probably better that way. I'd hate for Angus to get hurt too. I don't think the poor guy could survive a jump from a moving car."

"Aye. He willnae be driving anywhere until I can ensure his brakes were no' tampered with." The thought of anything happening to Angus or Mavis had him clenching and unclenching his fists.

Collin gestured back toward the castle and began to lead her in the middle of the barely traveled rocky road. It would have been quicker to hike through the forest layered with unruly heather, but her first sneeze struck that route home from their list.

Collin pulled the ruby broach from his pocket and handed it to her. "I found this at the cliff's edge when I saved you earlier."

"The color of your rival." She grinned.

"Aye, I guess it is."

"I'm sure most women like jewels no matter the color. I have a ruby bracelet but I'd never be a McDougall."

"Aye, you are no McDougall."

"About the cliff..." She took the pendant and chewed her bottom lip as if she was trying to find the right words. Her usual boisterous demeanor shifted to something more contemplative, a look that he wasn't used to seeing on her. "The thing is... I didn't slip."

Her words muddled his brain and took a minute to register. He eased her to stop walking. "If you dinnae slip, then what?"

"Someone pushed me. I felt the hand on my back, and then next thing I knew, the rock saved me from swimming with Nessie."

His muscles tensed at the thought. It was unthinkable that someone would want her dead. She hadn't been in town long enough to make enemies. "Did you see their face? Hear anything?"

"No." She held out the broach. "Maybe whoever it was dropped that little gem. Any idea who owns it?"

They glanced down at the exquisite stone that he'd once thought beautiful but was now somehow lacking its luster. "I've seen it before, but I donae remember where."

He moved closer to her, unfastened the pin, and attached it to her shirt.

"Aww...is that a token to remember the experience?" She glanced up at him with a raised brow.

"Nay, luv. Wear it as a badge of survival. Whoever it belongs to will think twice about trying again."

"I like the way you think, big guy." She patted his chest. "Kind of like a 'screw you' to the killer."

Her words made him smile, even though his heart clenched. He'd thought she was here to play out the curse, but what if the death the curse alluded to was hers? He bit back the anger and clenched his fists, vowing that the killer wouldn't get another chance.

Chapter 10

Collin and Angus checked the Town Car's brakes before Collin sent Angus into town to pick up Quinn's things and an order Collin had placed at a small boutique for additional clothes. Silence hung between them as she tried to process what had happened. She'd almost died, and the killer seemed unconcerned about extra casualties. No one was safe.

He'd escorted her to the room to shower and change, like the personal security of a celebrity, before disappearing to make some calls. After her shower, she walked out into the room to find her luggage and bags of new clothes sitting on the bed.

Quinn's vow to solve the mystery weighed heavy on her chest. If she didn't, someone could get hurt. Her lips pinched together as she rubbed her neck, replaying everything in her mind that had happened to try and figure out what, if anything, she'd missed.

She was standing in her bra and underwear, absently digging through her suitcase when the door flew open, pulling her from her thoughts. Collin entered the room. His gaze met hers and dropped from her eyes to her shoulders to her breasts, slowly and seductively sliding down the remainder of her body. The air around her seemed to dance with sparks from an invisible electric charge, and she felt a ripple of excitement. "Do you like what you see?"

"I...uh. I'm sorry to interrupt. I should have knocked." Collin crossed the threshold with a tray in his hands and shut the door behind him. She should have kicked him out, or clutched clothes to cover her nearly naked body, but all her inhibitions had diminished with her two near-death experiences. Who was she kidding? Inhibitions ranked right up there on her list with vegetables. She didn't like either.

He watched her seductively, his aura pulsing with need, as he crossed the room to sit the tray on the dresser. He cleared his throat to speak. "Mavis heard about our mishap and wanted me to bring these up. Her way of apologizing for the accident."

"She wasn't responsible." Quinn took a cookie off the plate and bit into it. "But I'll never turn away her cookies." She smiled and ate the cookie while pulling some clothes from her bag.

Collin moved behind her. He rested a warm palm on her arm, sending a shock of need and desire coiling through her body. In any other place, she might have thrown herself at him. The thought had crossed her mind.

He placed a tender kiss on her neck, making her sigh in pleasure. The prolonged anticipation to see what he'd do next was almost unbearable. Her pulse quickened in response to the feel of his lips. Had it been so long since she'd had her needs sated?

"Is that your way of apologizing for the accident?"

"Aye, you're beautiful, Quinn."

Quinn licked her dry lips. His words sent a tingle of need coursing through her body. She craved more, silently wondering how far he'd let things go.

"I almost died *twice* in your country," she teased, hoping he'd take the hint.

His hands moved to her hips, and he pulled her flush against his body, wrapping her in a seductive warmth. His heated breath traveled up the column of her neck as he placed kisses against her skin.

She knew the Highlander had a brain, and from the feel of him, he had a lot more notable attributes she would like to explore before saying goodbye to his motherland.

Quinn dropped the clothes back into her bag. She didn't need them...yet.

"I can kiss all your wounds."

Her momma would have been appalled at the dirty thoughts coursing through her mind. Her sisters would want a play-by-play. Quinn reached between their bodies and ran her hand over his jean-covered crotch. "This would be easier if you had on your skirt."

"Next time," he whispered before spinning her in his arms and crushing his lips against hers. He tasted of chocolate chip cookies. She smiled against his lips.

"You stole a cookie," she whispered. Her voice came out husky and wanting as his lips traveled down the other side of her neck while one hand moved to unhook her bra.

"I plan to steal a lot more than your cookies," he said as the bra slid to the floor. His gaze landed on the cuts on her chest from the car incident, and it was as if someone flipped a switch. His touch gentled, and his brows dipped.

Gone was the brazen Highlander who looked ready to ravish her. Her cheeks heated as she watched him slowly pull away. The cuts on her chest vaporized her chances of joining the foreign affair touchdown club. Surely they had something similar to the mile-high club but for tourists who were looking to score.

"I'm sorry." He dropped his hold and took a step back, putting more space between them and breaking whatever hold he'd had over her. "I donae know what came over me." He met her gaze. "When I'm near you, I cannae help myself."

"Why would you want to?" She had two choices. One to let him walk out the door and let her libido die down to a simmer or the second...to finish stripping and get the extra points.

The decision was ripped away when he turned and stormed out the door, leaving her trying to calm her racing heart.

"Nice...my first play was a fumble." Quinn was left hot and bothered. She couldn't deny she wanted him and wouldn't turn him away. Two more minutes and Collin would have gotten more than a simple thank-you for delivering her cookies. It wasn't as though he would have been a one-night stand. More like several nights, had she gotten her way. Sleeping with him would have been a more pleasant way to pass the time than trying to unravel a curse she didn't believe in. She needed to get to the bottom of things and quick. It was time she had her chat with Gwinnie, and she knew just where to find her.

After dressing, she wound her way through the castle, ignoring the look of hatred from the blonde Barbie as she passed. She'd started up the small staircase, taking two steps at a time, but by the time she reached the top, she was gasping for air and clutching her side. Her desire to talk to the ghost slowly dwindled with each step. The door to the tower stood open. Gwinnie herself stood in the middle of the room as Quinn entered. The apparition pointed toward the painting leaning up against the wall. A satin-dressed version of Quinn stared back at herself. A shiver skirted down her spine as she gazed upon it, inspecting each paint stroke. A ruby comb poked out of the unruly red hair. The woman in the painting had Quinn's mother's eyes and her father's cheekbones. The lady in the picture could have been Quinn's twin.

Quinn shook her head. This was impossible. She didn't believe in curses. "Your gypsy was a medium. She must have actually seen me coming."

"Aye," the ghost answered. "She did, and you must leave."

"Why?" Quinn asked, yanking the sheets off the other paintings that Collin had told her about to get an overall picture of what the medium had seen.

"They must never know how the emerald disappeared. Some mysteries are never meant to be solved."

"I hate to break it to you, lady, but I plan to figure this out." Quinn turned to find that Gwinnie vanished, replaced by the big, brooding, red-bearded Highlander.

"'Tis better if you leave the sins of the past where they lie to save your own life."

Quinn tilted her head and crossed her arms over her chest. "Why is everyone trying so hard to get me to leave? Your warning is a little late, by the way. Someone has already tried to kill me twice, and I'm still kicking." Quinn turned back to the paintings and slowly moved down each one until she stood in front of the one depicting someone handing over the stone to an unseen person. Both hands in the picture were those of men. "Help me solve this."

The ghost shimmered to hover beside her, leaving the entire right side of her body ice cold. "You'd risk your life for the Menzie name?"

"I don't know about that, but my momma didn't raise me to run from my issues, and she did have the common sense to teach me right from wrong. There is something real and wrong going on here, which someone is willing to kill for, and I plan to find out exactly what it is."

"You could die," he grumbled as he studied her. Interest twinkled in his eyes, as if he was sizing her up for the challenge ahead.

"And Scotland could be overrun with pizza joints. Are you going to help me?"

His hardened gaze narrowed onto hers, so she mimicked his look. If he thought a simple disgruntled look would dissuade her, he'd never met her family.

"Find this book and you'll find your answers, but donae say I dinnae warn you." He swished over to the third painting of an old library. He gestured to one of the books in particular, making her step closer. The faded black, worn-out spine had symbols down the length instead of words.

"What does it mean?" she asked and turned to find Redbeard had vanished.

"What is it with you Scotts needing better manners?" Quinn yelled out just as Collin walked into the room.

"Who you yelling at, luv?" he asked, gazing around the empty room.

"Redbeard, your relative."

"Ah." He gave a slow nod. "You might have a point then. His mother ruled the castle with an iron fist. It's said that the staff and nobles alike were afraid of her."

"So, Redbeard's mom was Gwinnie's mother-in-law? Gwinnie and he were married?"

"Aye."

"That explains a lot," Quinn said, grabbing the sheets and recovering the pictures.

"Quinn." Collin rested a gentle hand on her arm. "We should talk about what happened in your chamber."

"Nothing to say. For a brief minute, you wanted me. I saw the need in your eyes, but it's fine. My sexy American awesomeness scared you. It happens. It's okay, really." She smiled up at him, even though the wall around her heart had a new fissure. "I'm arm candy to ward off Blondie. There's no need to pretend behind closed doors."

"That's no' it." Collin's voice lowered to a deep timbre. "You've almost died twice since you've been here. I cannae seem to stop the attacks, but if I bed you, I'll be even more distracted. Maybe 'tis best if Angus drives you over to the next town where there's lodging, and maybe you'll be safe. I cannae help but feel getting you away from the castle would redirect the attacks."

Quinn rolled her eyes and patted his chest. She couldn't help it. He was like a new toy that she'd been told not to play with. "First of all, you helped me up the cliff; I'll give you that, but I didn't die the first time or the second. Ye of little faith. But if you want me gone, I'll go."

"This isnae about what I want. I'm trying to do the right thing."

"So am I considering I'm stuck on your mothership and you have my face painted on canvas like your own personal Guinevere. I'm going to do the right thing and help you." She patted his chest. "So it's settled. I'm staying." Quinn sidestepped him and sashayed out of the room with a little more sway in her steps, teasing and taunting him with her assets, which he'd denied himself the pleasure of getting to know better.

He followed as she jogged down the steps and made her way into the main entrance hall where she was halted by a parade of men carrying tables and chairs toward the ballroom. She'd forgotten all about the party.

"Come with me." Collin caught up to her and took her hand, pulling Quinn toward the kitchen and out the back entrance where she'd tried to use her cellphone.

"You need better cell service," she announced out of the blue.

"I need a lot of things," he countered with a glance over his shoulder as he continued pulling her toward a little house on the property.

"Who lives there?" she asked, slipping her fingers free.

"Garth, the caretaker, but that's no' where we're going."

A seven-foot, big, burly man stepped out of the worn shack with an ax in his grip. Harness, the white-haired dog, was by his side. A long, dark beard hung down the man's flannel shirt, and his dark gaze watched them. He reminded her of a cross between a lumberjack and a serial killer, and by the way he was looking at them, she guessed the latter. Quinn stumbled, and Collin caught her arm before she fell flat on her face.

She followed Collin and climbed the little Mt. Everest, wondering where on earth he was taking her. They crossed the bridge and entered the clearing where she'd seen him the first time on horseback. Her nose twitched in anticipation of nature surrounding her.

"I'm not going into the forest." She stopped and propped a hand on her hip.

Suffering from hayfever was not on her agenda for the night.

He let out a resigned sigh before sweeping her up into his arms. She could have protested if she'd wanted, but she didn't bother. It wasn't every day she was pressed up against a hard, manly chest. If nothing else, she'd remember the feeling and use it as material for her dreams.

"I'd never take you into the forest."

Collin headed to the end of the clearing, where a small house, identical to the caretaker's, sat. He lowered Quinn to her feet, letting her soft body slide down his length. His hard-on pressed against the apex of her thighs as he opened the door and ushered her inside.

She expected cobwebs, dust, and worse, but the small cabin was as clean as the room she was staying in. The furnishings were humble and made of solid wood, the cooking items antique. She loved every part of the small little house down to the beautiful blue quilt folded at the foot of the bed.

Quinn picked up the soft quilt. The silky material surprised her. "Who's place is this?"

"This belonged to Gwinnie's ancestors. Her father was the castle steward, and she fell in love with the laird. It's been updated some through the years."

Quinn couldn't imagine the ghost in the north tower wearing anything other than the jewels and satin that she'd seen her wearing.

She dropped the quilt and smoothed the lines. "Why did you bring me here?"

He closed the distance between them and cupped her cheek, resting his forehead against hers. "You're stubborn."

"And?" If there was a punch line, she was missing it.

"Beautiful." He placed a tender kiss to her lips.

"And?" She was still confused, but she enjoyed the lip action, and he didn't appear to be moving.

"You're outspoken, a pain in my ass, and American."

Her lips twisted into a smile. The big Highlander was actually getting to know her. "You've giving me whiplash. One minute, you look like you want to devour me, and the next minute, you're acting like I'm the one with the measles. So what's it going to be this time, big guy?"

"I brought you here so we wouldnae be disturbed."

She chuckled, making his brows dip. "Is this like your love shack? Do you bring all of the girls here and sweet talk them?"

"I've never brought another here."

"Why did you walk out of my room?" Quinn couldn't help herself from asking in an effort to figure out what made him tick, and it didn't hurt that teasing the Highlander was just too easy.

"I was trying to be a gentleman."

"I'm not a lady." Her grin grew as she lifted her shirt over her head and dropped it on the floor. "And I'm not afraid to take what I want."

She reached behind her back and unhooked her bra, letting it slide off her shoulders and down to the floor. She gestured to the scratches and cuts on her chest. "This happened. I survived, and it hasn't swayed me from wanting you. Can you deal with this?"

"Aye." Collin's voice grew husky as he lifted her into his arms. A girly yelp escaped her lips before she could rein it back.

He laid Quinn on the bed, and her heart beat frantically as heat pooled between her thighs. She was embarrassingly wet and wanting, but nothing was going to stop her this time.

She kicked off her tennis shoes onto the floor in anticipation and had reached for the button on her jeans before he placed his hand over hers and took over. He kissed her stomach as his fingers made quick work of the fastening. The sound of her zipper lowering filled the quietness of the room. Her quickened breath was loud in her ears. He eased the jeans down her legs. His lips followed the path, kissing her everywhere but where she wanted most.

She lay naked as he stood tall in front of her, taking his time to undress for her visual excitement. His blue eyes darkened and hooded as he licked his lips, never taking his eyes from her body. He crawled up and settled between her thighs. *Now, this is what I'm talking about.*

Quinn raked her nails slowly over his tan back and held his gaze. The rapid rise and fall of his chest matched hers as he reached between them and grabbed his shaft, running the stiff length between her wet folds. No words mattered in that minute, no curse, no emerald. It was just him and her, both mindless with pleasure, as he slid deep inside and took her over the edge, straight into amazing bliss.

Chapter 11

Collin woke to moonlight streaming in through the small window. The satin quilt covered them from the waist down. Quinn lay asleep in his arms. A few scratches covered the creamy contours of her back. Collin basked in her beauty, knowing that even though their time was limited, he still wouldn't have changed what happened. He could no longer deny the sparks, even if it meant sticking by her side the remainder of her stay. No other harm would come to her. He wouldn't let it.

"Get out of your head," she mumbled, and he glanced down at her face to find her looking up at him. A lazy smile covered her lips before she kissed his chest. "Don't overthink it, stud. It was sex, not a declaration of love."

"Isnae that supposed to be my line?" He pressed a kiss to her lips as her stomach growled.

"I don't suppose you thought ahead to bring my cookies?"

Collin rolled on top of her, pressing his body into hers for one last kiss before getting out of the bed. He picked up her clothes and tossed them to her before pulling on his own clothes. "I figured we'd save them for dessert in the room." He winked as he fastened his pants. "Right now, I'm going to make us a midnight snack."

Her eyes widened and she held her hand to her chest. "You cook? That kind of ruins your manly image."

He chuckled. "Even us manly types need to eat, right?"

"I suppose. But do you cook in your skirt?" she asked, getting off the bed and shimmying into her panties and bra.

"Only on special occasions." Quinn finished getting dressed and Collin linked his fingers through hers and led her out into the moonlight.

He warmed up leftovers and fed her properly before taking her cookies to his room and Quinn to his bed. Exhausted, with a full belly and feeling sated, she slept in his arms until the early morning hours.

Collin left Quinn sound asleep in his room as he jogged down the stairs and into the kitchen. He grabbed a piece of bacon, crunching into the crispy goodness, then winked at Mavis, making her smile.

"Someone is in a good mood. I donae suppose it has anything to do with a certain American."

"She's great, isnae she?"

"Aye, I like her very much. But, Collin Menzie, I love you like a son, and you should remember that she'll be leaving soon."

Her words deflated his sails. She meant well and true, Collin did know Quinn would be leaving soon, but she was here now, and that was all that mattered.

"Someone pushed her over the cliff yesterday."

Mavis paused mid-stir and shot her gaze to Collins. "Who?"

He shrugged. That was the million-dollar question. "Someone disnae want her here."

"There's only one someone I can think of," Mavis said and resumed stirring. "Margarete. Which reminds me, she was looking for you last night." Mavis pointed her spoon in his direction. "You should be wary of that one. She's like a vulture, she is."

"Speaking of Margarete, she dinnae attack me when I came downstairs. Where is she hiding?"

"Ah...you two must be talking about Margarete," Angus said, walking into the room. He grabbed a biscuit and kissed Mavis on the cheek. "I passed her this morning on her way out. She said she had a meeting in town but that she'd be back by the party. She also said she gave the workers the weekend off so they wouldnae be in the way."

"The party." Damn, he'd forgotten about that. "I need to call the boutique. Quinn's going to need a dress."

"And whose colors will she be wearin'?" Mavis asked.

"Mine." The answer was quick and automatic. The thought of seeing her in any other plaid made his stomach clench. All of the women would be dressed in the clan colors they represented. The boutique dressed both clans for just this occasion.

Mavis chuckled. "She disnae need a dress. She has one."

Collin's brows dipped as he stared at her.

"It was made special just for her. Donnae you remember?"

A smile split his lips. His heart skipped a beat just thinking about seeing Quinn in the antique dress. She'd be the vision in the portrait.

"Donae be ridiculous, Mavis. She cannae wear that old thing. I can take her into town to try some on. Where is the lassie?" Angus asked.

"She's sleeping. The dress should fit Quinn, but Mavis, please call the tailor and have him on standby just in case."

"And how would you know what size she wears?" Mavis asked.

Collin couldn't contain his grin. Even though a gentleman never kissed and told, Collin knew Angus could read the answer on his face. He grabbed another piece of bacon before leaving them to head into his office.

Collin plopped down in his da's old chair. Thinking of him made Collin's gut clench. His da would have never let anyone staying under his roof get hurt, least of all Collin's mom, while he was laird. Quinn would look like the lady of the house in the finest silk money could buy in that special dress, which was fit for a queen. She would be the lady tonight, the one she claimed not to be last night. How had she put it? She'd not only be the arm candy by his side, but so much more.

Collin whistled while working on the growing pile of bills and paperwork that Ramsey had left on his desk. Not even the mundane busywork could ruin his morning. A soft knock sounded on the office door as he worked his way through the middle of his stack.

"Enter," he yelled, expecting to be greeted with Quinn's smiling face, not Abigail.

"I'm sorry to disturb you, but Laird McDougall called and said you're late."

"Bloody hell." Collin tossed the pen down. He'd been so preoccupied with thoughts of Quinn that he'd forgotten about meeting Ian at the pub to go over the list attending tonight's party. "Tell Angus to meet me out front in ten minutes."

"Yes, sir. And Mr. Ramsey wanted me to tell you he took the emerald to the appraiser for insurance purposes and has submitted a claim for your truck."

"Thank you."

She nodded and left just as quickly as she had entered.

Collin took the back stairs up to his room to find Quinn sleeping peacefully. He hated to disturb her, but he didn't want her waking up and thinking he'd abandoned her, so he kissed her cheek. "Quinn, luv."

She turned toward his voice and greeted him with a smile before she opened her eyes. "If you didn't come bearing cookies or muffins, go away."

"I have to run into town and meet Ian about the party tonight. Do you want to go with me?"

"To meet Ian and ruin my morning?" She shook her head and turned, snuggling into the pillow. "No, I'm good."

"Yes, you are." Collin ran his hand up her arm and placed a tender kiss on her flesh.

"Be careful," she mumbled as he walked to the door.

"Please, donae leave the castle until I return," he called back even as apprehension sat like a boulder in his gut.

She shot up and stared at him, teasing him with the sight of her breasts. The decision to stay warred with his duty to leave. He expected her to accuse him of being a caveman or something worse, and instead, she smiled a little too sweetly. "I'll be in the library all day."

"Promise?"

"Of course. Tell Ian I send my regards."

Collin chuckled and opened the door, waiting until the last minute to look back, partly because he wanted to remember the vision of her well sated and lying naked in his bed. "He'll never believe it."

"Well, then tell him I said to bite my ass." She grinned cheerfully.

"That he'll believe." Collin winked and shut the door.

Chapter 12

Quinn plopped back against the satin sheets and clutched them to her chest. She hadn't lied about the library. She was going to find that book if it was the last thing she did. Collin might not understand. No, he'd be pissed if he knew she was hunting the answers to questions she didn't even know to ask. All she knew was that the book held the key, and she was going to find it.

Renewed enthusiasm propelled her out of the bed and into her clothes. A quick shower in her room and change of clothes would get rid of the cobwebs in her head, not to mention ease her deliciously sated body. If she'd made a bucket list, she would have been able to cross off several touchdowns.

She left Collin's room, opened the door to her room, and froze with her hand still gripping the knob. A copy of a newspaper clipping she knew all too well was stuck to the wall with a knife. "Son of a bitch."

Quinn hurried to close the door and glanced around the room. Everything else was in place but a few pieces of clothes that were hanging out of her suitcase. Someone had violated her space. Anger strummed through her body like an agitated wasp nest. She moved cautiously through the room to the knife sticking in the picture of her head and yanked it free, catching the paper as it fell. The picture was of her when her ex-fiancé Danny had died.

Unlike the copy in her apartment, this one had the eyes gouged out and a red mark across her neck. She was more surprised that someone had gone to the trouble to find a copy of the article than she was that someone wanted her dead. Had Collin seen this? Surely he would have said something before letting her seduce him. The article had tainted her as a fraud and black widow after the event.

Her space had been violated, her past on display, and whoever was responsible was playing a deadly game that they would not win. They thought this would scare her. Not by a long shot. She smiled and narrowed her eyes.

After showering and dressing, Quinn jogged down the stairs and into the kitchen to grab a blueberry muffin. Mavis was behind the stove.

"Well, good mornin', Quinn. How are you on this fine day?" Mavis asked like a mom who knew Quinn had spent the night having the best sex of her life.

"Wonderful as usual, now that I have your muffin." Quinn raised the muffin and took a bite, letting the blueberry flavor fill her mouth. "Can I ask you something, hypothetically?" She covered her mouth and mumbled, not wanting to give her a show of the food in her mouth. Mom would be proud.

"Sure, dear." She leaned against the counter.

Quinn swallowed. "If I wanted to learn more about Gwinnie, where would I go?"

"Ahh. You're still trying to figure out the curse, arenae you?"

Quinn shrugged. "Well considering someone painted my face into one of the starring roles, I thought I'd give it a good go."

Mavis wiped her hands on her apron. "Follow me."

Quinn should have known that Mavis would have the answers, cook or not, so she followed slowly behind, leaving the confines of the kitchen to another spiral staircase. Mavis surprised Quinn with her agility on the steps. Just when Quinn was certain they were headed toward the tower, Mavis turned in the opposite direction toward the fire-stricken part of the castle.

"Collin only keeps some of the relics in the ballroom, but not all."

"No?"

She threw open a pair of double doors, seemingly untouched by the fire, and stepped aside, watching Quinn's face.

Her mouth dropped open as she walked into a beautiful room with the finest of silks and silver. Antique furniture filled the walls, along with tapestries, and the finest of carpets covered the floor. Quinn stepped over to the closest mannequin and ran her fingers over the dress covering it. It was the same dress in the portrait. "The portrait doesn't do this dress justice. It's stunning."

"It's yours. Made and designed by Lady Menzie, after the portraits were commissioned, for the woman who returned the emerald."

"Gwinnie?" Quinn asked.

"No, her mother-in-law."

"Noooo." A smile split her lips. "Old Iron Fist did this?"

"She did." Mavis walked over to the mannequin and held out the skirt. "And it looks like it will fit."

A special garter sat on the mannequin's leg beneath the skirt. It held a blade, encased in a sheath, with an emerald encrusted gem handle.

Mavis slipped the handle free and held out a dagger. "She had a smaller emerald placed in the handle above the blade as a token of appreciation for whoever returned the emerald. She gave a matching one to the psychic who foretold your coming."

"Seriously?" Iron Fist was sentimental? "Have you heard any tales about what happened to the psychic?" Quinn asked, moving around the room taking in all the beautiful pieces.

"She stayed, worked for the mistress and handed down her blade to the women in her line."

Her words made Quinn pause and then turn to face Mavis. "Are her relatives still here in town?"

Mavis smiled and lifted her skirt, pulling a dagger from her leg holster. "As a matter of fact, we are."

She dropped her skirt.

"You're a psychic?" Quinn asked.

"'Tis true."

"Did you see me coming?" Quinn asked, stepping over to her; she took the woman's hand, feeling an instant kinship from one weirdo to another.

"I did, and when Angus told me he was picking you up, I dinnae know if I should be mortified at what it meant or excited that you were real."

"So you know the secrets of the curse?"

"No, dear. I only know what was told to me by my ancestors and the reasoning behind this dress. Lady Menzie took ill no' too long after the emerald went missing, and Laird Menzie, along with the rest of the castle, mourned her loss."

Everyone must have thought Lady Menzie had lost her mind to believe in psychics and God knows what else. Quinn was surprised someone back in those days didn't think Lady Menzie was a devil worshiper for even employing someone who could tell the future. Quinn's respect for the Menzies was growing on a daily basis. They were kind, caring and crazy, just like Quinn.

"Collin wants me to call the tailor if the dress disnae fit you for the dance tonight."

"He wants me to wear that?" Quinn turned back to the beautiful garment and eyed it with renewed interest. Tilting her head, she let her gaze travel over the beautiful piece of art and the exquisite detail put into making it. The dress would fit, even if she had to wear multiple layers of Spanx and gobs of butter to slide that sucker on. That bitch was hers.

"Aye," Mavis answered, walking to the back of the mannequin and untying the corset. "Strip and let's see if it fits."

Ten minutes later, Quinn stood in front of a floor-length mirror in the room inhaling little breaths. The tightness of the corset made it difficult to breathe, but it sure did make her breasts look fabulous.

Quinn grabbed her boobs and grinned. "Margarete only wishes she had these babies."

"I'm sure Collin is pleased with them as well."

Quinn blushed, not from Mavis' comments, but from remembering just how pleased Collin had been.

"You look lovely, dear, and it fits perfectly," Mavis said, coming to stand beside Quinn.

"I'll be lucky if I don't pass out."

"You'll live," Mavis said, moving behind her to untie the torture device. "And you'll be the prettiest Menzie at the ball."

"I'm not a Menzie," Quinn corrected her.

"No' yet."

"I'll tell you what. You learn to make pizza, and I'll consider coming back to visit, as long as you promise I won't have to eat haggis." Quinn chuckled, relieved her lungs had expanded as the garment loosened.

Quinn slipped back into her clothes as Mavis held the dress. "I'll get this steamed and leave it in your room."

Her room. Her room where the knife-wielding killer had been. "Uh...can you just leave it in Collin's room?"

"Of course, dear. I just dinnae want to assume."

"No assuming. I slept there last night, and apparently, someone entered my room while we were busy." Multiple orgasms busy. She kept that comment to herself.

"Oh dear." Her brows dipped, and her lips turned down. "Have you told Collin?"

Telling Collin would require a deeper conversation about the message that was left. Quinn still hadn't decided what, if anything, to tell him. Her past was her past. She was proud of many things in her life, but Danny's death wasn't one of them. "Not yet. I don't want to worry him."

Mavis rested her palm on Quinn's arm. "Trust Collin. He's a good man."

Quinn pasted her most sincere look on her face, which she normally reserved for funerals and her mother. "I do and I will, just not today. This party is a big deal for both clans, and I don't want to start another clan war when he starts accusing everyone within earshot. Next thing you know, someone else will be painting a picture depicting me as the charlatan capable of breaking the bridge over the great divide. No, I think I'll wait."

The dress, along with the ruby broach, would be enough to incite an attack. An attack she could handle. Talking about the skeletons in her own closet? Not so much. Quinn turned to leave and paused at the door. "Can you make sure the dagger and sheath are included with the dress?

"Of course."

"Thank you for this, and your secret."

"All of my ancestors before me have taken care of the lady of the house. You might not officially be a Menzie, but you are the lady of *this* house. The returned emerald confirms it." Mavis smiled as if she knew something Quinn didn't.

The woman was a bit delusional, but who was Quinn to call her out on the misconception? Quinn had done a good deed and returned the emerald. It wasn't as though she'd come riding in on a white horse with a sword to slay a dragon.

Quinn gestured with her thumb over her shoulder. "I'll be in the library if anyone needs me."

"I'll send in cookies and refreshments."

An endless supply of cookies from Mavis, delusional though she may be, might have been worth the whole trip. Not to mention the sexy Highlander whose touch made her body sizzle. "Thanks."

Quinn entered the humongous library. New and old books covered the floor-to-ceiling shelves. She stood overwhelmed by the sheer volume of books that waited. It was going to take her all day to find the magical book with the answers. A road map would have been nice.

Hours later, with a cookie in hand, she had cleared one wall looking for the intricate spine when she spotted a shadow by the door. She turned, and her heart stilled. Quinn clutched the cookie to her chest as if it would stop her impending heart attack.

The caretaker, Garth, stood on the threshold, blocking the entrance with his hands behind his back. She held his gaze, afraid to move, hell, afraid to breathe. That man could snap her like a twig. Without a word, he stepped into the room and came right toward her.

Quinn lifted her chin and refused to cower. "I'm Quinn."

"I know who you are," he answered in a deep, dark voice with his hands clutched behind his back. Did he have an ax ready to slice her in two? "You're the one causing quite a stir."

"Now listen here, you big lumberjack..." The words died on her lips as he moved closer, pinning her back

DEADLY INTENT

against the wooden shelves. The sharp angles of the shelves and hard spines pressed into her skin. He reached over her head and slid a book back into place before grabbing another one.

He narrowed his eyes down at her and sniffed her hair before stepping back.

Okay, weird man had a scent fetish. Quinn restrained the urge to sniff her hair to figure out what he could have smelled. Instead, her gaze went to the romance novel in his hand. It was one that had bored her to tears. Quinn took the book from him and shoved it back into its place, walked to the wall on the right, and grabbed a better one. She held it out. "This is one of my favorites, but the sequel isn't due out for another few months. You can thank me later."

"You liked that one?" he asked while flipping the book over to read the back.

"Yeah, it's got romance, mystery, and intrigue. Give it a try."

"You like this author?"

She smiled trying to ease the tension in the room. "Yeah, he's good. You know, you two would look alike if it wasn't for the beard and clothes. Do you have a twin that lives in the states?"

"Nay."

She shrugged. "I guess they say everyone has a doppelganger. Yours happens to write romance. Enjoy the book."

"You Americans are pushy."

"Not all Americans, just me." What a jackass. Still a jackass that had access to an ax. Maybe she should have let him read the boring book, but hopefully, the new one might hold his interest longer, which sounded like a much better plan. A busy reader was too busy to chase her while swinging an ax to cut her into tiny pieces. Quinn had a brain. Regardless of what her sisters thought.

Garth left without another word, and her racing heart slowed. She spent the rest of the afternoon in the damn library, checking the spines for a book that wasn't even in the room. She stood at the window watching the sun dip below the horizon. The book was a lost cause, making her heart sink into her toes. Would she even have time to figure out who was trying to kill her before they succeeded? Shoulders slumped, Quinn went back to Collin's room to get ready and dress for the dance.

Chapter 13

Collin walked into his room to find Quinn standing as a vision of beauty in his colors. His heart quickened at the sight, and his cock strained against his jeans. It wasn't just the dress she was wearing that took his breath away—although her breasts were a sight—it was the stunning woman in the dress. A smile split her lips even as her creamy flesh called to be kissed. Her red hair was curled and styled on her head, and she was a vision.

"I look hot, right?" She smiled.

He couldn't answer. His breath was stolen, but not his resolve. Instead, he kicked the door closed with his boot and crossed the room to her, pressing his lips to hers in a deep, soul-searing kiss of approval.

Collin slipped the clip in her hair free, letting the soft red tendrils fall down her back. "I'll take that as a yes." She gave him a saucy wink. "We're going to be late."

"Aye, that we are." Collin bunched the silky material in his hands and lifted the fabric up her thighs in search of the gold hidden beneath. Cupping her cheeks, he lifted her bare ass onto the dresser, making sure not to ruin the dress. Pressing his legs between her thighs, he moved in closer.

"You're beautiful," he whispered against her chest as he kissed each mound. She popped the buttons on his jeans and unzipped them. Her warm hand stroked his length, making a guttural groan slip free.

"It's the dress, isn't it?" she asked with a wicked smile playing on her lips.

"No, luv." Collin placed his palm on her cheek. "It's the woman in the dress."

"Right answer." She pulled him closer and positioned his cock between her folds.

The vixen wasn't even wearing a thong. She was wet and ready. If he could have lowered her corset with his teeth, he would have loved to suck the sweet berries that were hidden beneath. The damn thing wouldn't budge.

"You can play later," she whispered in his ear before nibbling.

He slid inside her tight sheath, seating himself to the hilt. Her head lulled back, and her eyes closed, even as her fingernails dug into his skin. She wanted this as much as he wanted to give it to her. "Ah...luv, you feel so good."

Collin's hands slid up her thighs, stopping when he found a single barrier on her right leg. He lifted the skirt higher to see. The emerald-encrusted knife was inside the sleeve, and the sight made his cock twitch.

"You like that?"

He slid out and thrust inside her again.

"Oh fuck me." She moaned. "You keep doing that, and I'll wear it later while I'm naked."

Her promise spurred on his primal passion. Visions of her naked in his bed, wearing nothing more than a weapon strapped to her creamy thigh, made his balls tighten in anticipation.

He moved his hand to her small bud. He wasn't going to last long. Not with the way her body was clenching him tight. Her need spiraled his to new heights. He swirled her clit with his finger as he moved inside her, taking her with every fiber of his being. His muscles clenched as sweat beaded his brow. Her channel tightened, pulling him over the edge. He pressed on her bud and took them both over the edge as he soaked her with his seed.

He stayed inside her. The rise and fall of her chest matched his own as they slowed. He placed a tender kiss on her lips. "Donae move."

She smiled. "Are you telling me what to do?"

Collin moved the dress to where she was holding it in her hands.

"I donae want you to ruin your dress. Donae move until I clean you up."

Collin pulled his boxers up and refastened his jeans before going to the bathroom and returning with a washcloth to clean her up. The move was as intimate as when he'd been inside of her. If he didn't hurry, he'd be hard and taking her again, and they'd never get to the party.

Collin lifted her off the dresser, letting her soft curves slide down his body, kissing her lips when she was on her feet. "Give me fifteen minutes and we'll go down together."

"Take your time. It's going to take longer than fifteen minutes for me to get my hair back up in that clip."

"You should wear it down. You look like an angel." He winked, unable to walk away. He kissed her plump lips again before getting in the shower.

Quinn Thatcher was growing on him. The American had not only returned his family's emerald but she'd also chipped away at his guarded heart. He couldn't deny that he was falling for her. The thought of her leaving left a sour taste in his mouth. He didn't wish her pilot ill, but hoped he'd take a bit longer to recover. Collin dressed in his kilt and stepped out of the room to find Quinn sitting on the bed. The news article that had been inside his desk was in her hands, and his heart stopped.

"Where did you get that?" He knew the answer, yet still he asked.

"It was stuck to the wall in my bedroom this morning." She handed it to him. The picture in the article had her eyes cut out and a red mark across her throat. Someone had altered the picture he'd tucked away.

Collin's entire body tensed as he crinkled the paper in his hands. "Someone's been in my office."

"What?" She bolted up. "You knew? Why didn't you say anything?" Quinn crossed her arms beneath her breasts, lifting them even higher.

She snapped her fingers and pointed to her eyes. "Answer me."

"It was no' important. Did you expect me no' to know who was staying beneath

139

my roof? Besides, the article says you dinnae know he was going to die."

"I did know." Her face pinked as she narrowed her eyes. "I knew the precise moment he was going to die. It was the only premonition I've ever had. I can't explain how I knew; I just did, and I warned him. For weeks, I begged him to cancel his trip and not get on the plane. I tried everything I could to stop him, but he wouldn't listen. He thought I was crazy. He didn't understand, and he left, and just like in my vision; his plane ended up on the side of a mountain."

Collin's heart ached for the pain in Quinn's eyes. The vulnerability she was gifting to him was rare and contradicted the strength she portrayed.

He cupped her cheek and rested his forehead against hers. "I promise you that I will always listen and believe you no matter how crazy you sound."

"Someone is trying to kill me." Her voice wavered.

"Aye, and I willnae let them."

"I willnae let them," she echoed with a Scottish lilt. The resolve returned to her voice, the vulnerability she'd just showed replaced with determination, and that scared him worse.

Collin put on his boots and watched her in the mirror as she fastened the ruby to her dress. It didn't matter that the ruby was Ian's colors, but the reason why she'd put it on did matter. She was trying to anger a killer.

Bending her over the dresser, and taking her from behind until she agreed to take it off, might have entered his mind, but even then, he knew his victory would be short-lived. She'd find a way around her promise. Better to do it with him at her side than on her own.

"Ian will be pleased you're wearing his color."

Quinn rolled her eyes and met Collin's gaze in the reflection. "We both know why I'm wearing it, but I'm more a green kind of girl."

He stood from the bed and held out his hand. "Good answer."

Chapter 14

Quinn pasted the best debutant smile she could muster on her face as she eyed everyone as a potential enemy. Soft music played in the ballroom as men and women dressed in red and green plaid danced on the floor.

She hadn't expected so many people in green. Where had they been hiding this entire time?

Collin led her to a table up on a dais. Ian was already seated, along with a white-haired woman to his right. He locked eyes with them as they approached and gave a lopsided grin. "Is that little spec of red on her dress your way of saying Quinn is fair game?"

"I'm no one's game," Quinn answered, even as the muscles in Collin's arm bunched beneath her hold. "But if I were, my blood runs green."

"'Tis tradition the Menzies dance with the McDougalls." Ian jumped down from the platform and held out his hand.

"I'm sure the lady you were sitting with would like to dance."

Ian glanced over his shoulder and turned back with a smile. "My mom hates to dance."

"Come on, Quinn. It's tradition."

"That's a stupid tradition," Quinn grumbled.

"Aye, but it keeps incest out of the equation, and I know you want to set a good example for the others."

He gestured toward a table, where Quinn spotted Abigail sitting in a green dress, watching.

She ignored Ian's hand and stood on her tiptoes, planting a kiss on Collin's lips, leaving no doubt as to whose bed she'd be sleeping in later.

"I'll make sure to step on his toes." She winked, making Collin smile before she let Ian drag her to the dance floor.

Ian rested his hands on her waist as they slow danced. She watched as

Margarete was quick to fill her void. Her dress was impressive. It was sleek, hugged her curves and was the color of Collin's house. The sight had Quinn seeing red.

"Ne'er mind her, Quinn. She disnae hold a candle to you."

Collin held Quinn's gaze, and it was in that minute that she hoped Ian was right. Quinn stopped dancing and turned to Ian. "Who are you, and what did you do with Ian McDougall."

His laughter rang out, even as he started moving them both in the dance. "'Tis a shame you prefer green, Quinn Thatcher. I'd have been nicer to persuade you to my side."

"You don't know how to be nice." Quinn glanced over at Margarete, who had her arm wrapped around Collin's bicep as he read something in his hands. The man from breakfast the first morning stood next to Collin and was pointing at the paper. Had that guy been the one to inform Collin of her past? "Remind me again who's talking with Collin."

She turned to give Ian her full attention.

"My sister, Margarete, and Ramsey, Collin's financial advisor."

Quinn stopped dancing. "Margarete is a McDougall?"

"Aye."

"Why is she wearing green?" Quinn's voice rose, as did her temper.

Before he could answer, Abigail appeared by Quinn's side. "Excuse me, Quinn, but Mavis asked to see you in the kitchen."

"Thanks, Abby." Quinn turned back to Ian. "Ian, meet Abby. You two dance." Ian's brows dipped at her suggestion, making Quinn smile. "Set a good example." She patted him on the back as she left.

Abby blushed, even as Ian pulled her into his arms, quickly replacing Quinn. She made her way through the crowd toward the side entrance near the kitchen. Stepping out into the hallway, she inhaled a deep breath debating whether, if she tossed Margarete out by her hair, her actions would start another clan war.

"What the hell is wrong with me? I'm a strong, independent woman," Quinn mumbled as she entered the kitchen. The familiar smell of tomato sauce, herbs and spices drifted to her nose.

She spotted the pizza sitting on the counter. Her eyes widened in surprise. "You didn't."

"Aye, I did," Mavis smiled while slipping a slice onto a plate and handing it to Quinn.

"How did you have time to whip this together? I just mentioned it today."

"I saw it months ago in my visions. I had plenty of time to perfect it. It wasnae done in time, or I would have sent it to the library and you could have had it for lunch."

"The library was a bust. I expected old books, but they were mostly new. The one I was looking for has a black spine with white symbols on it, like in one of the portraits," Quinn said, as she took her first bite of the gooey goodness, a string of cheese hitting her in the chin as it broke free. She used her tongue to gather it without missing a beat.

"You should try the old library."

"Old library?" Quinn's interest piqued, but not enough to stop her from devouring the entire slice of pizza.

"Aye, it's in the east wing. Most of the books were covered with smoke from the fire, but none went up in flames."

Quinn grabbed a napkin and gestured to the pizza. "Hide that. I don't want to share."

Mavis chuckled as Quinn left the kitchen and headed toward the east wing. She took her time peeking into the rooms, unsure which was the library. A smoky smell lingered in the air as she pushed open some double doors. Black spines covered the bookshelves, and instantly she spotted the one she was looking for. Clarence stood next to the bookshelf, his arms folded over his ghostly body. "Donae do this."

"Hey, if it wasn't for you, I wouldn't be here at all."

"She gave my ancestors the emerald to have a better life, but it was cursed and bad things started happening so we locked it away. We couldnae sell it and have a clear conscious that the next owners wouldnae come to the same fate. You've returned the stone to the rightful heirs. You've done enough."

"I'm this close to figuring this out. I have to help Collin. Like your family not giving the stone away, because it was the right thing to do, so is this."

Clarence vanished out of sight as Quinn grabbed the book to pull it free. Only when she did, she heard a click. The book popped back into place, and the bookshelf opened back into the wall. "A secret passageway?"

Lifting her skirt, she stepped inside, and the bookshelf shut behind her, encasing her in darkness. Her heart raced as she felt along the wall for a lever or anything to reopen the door. She found nothing. She inhaled a deep breath of salty air and had taken a step farther inside when her foot kicked against something on the floor. She reached down, hoping it wasn't a dead body. Her hands felt the object and she breathed a silent sigh of relief. A flashlight.

"They didn't have these back in the day. Someone's been in here since this little baby was invented."

She flicked the switch, illuminating the stone passageway with light.

"Hello," she hollered. Her voice echoed as it bounced off the walls. A small breeze touched her cheek, relieving her fear that there was no ventilation. She slowly walked farther down the corridor as her heart hammered. Ghosts never scared her...but this place sent a shiver down her spine and left goosebumps on her arms.

Gwinnie from the north tower appeared. "I used this cave to help the poor."

Quinn stepped toward the opening and glanced down. It was easily ten feet to the rocks below. "I don't see how, unless you could fly."

"I sent down trinkets in the linens. Stuff that wouldn't be missed and that didn't mean anything to the Menzies but could change the lives of those in need."

"You were like a Robin Hood, but stealing from your own family," Quinn guessed and glanced around at the stuff in the tunnel. The items were newer, not from the century when Gwinnie lived. These were expensive items from today's day and time. Pieces of crystal, an expensive looking clock, and other odds and ends. "Looks like someone is carrying on your tradition."

Gwinnie shook her head. "Nay, this is an act of greed."

She vanished before Quinn could press her for a name. It didn't matter. She'd find out soon enough.

Chapter 15

Collin's stomach sank as he read the appraiser's report. The word "fake" stared back, mocking him. Had Quinn known the emerald wasn't real? "This cannae be."

"It is, Collin. I had him check the stone twice."

"I knew she was a fraud," Margarete whispered. "I bet she kept the real one. Collin, I'd never be that devious."

"Yes, you would." Collin shook her hold off his arm and searched the dance floor for Quinn. Instead, he spotted Ian with one of Collin's maid's in his arms. Collin stomped across the room. "Where is she?"

Ian dipped Abigail and brought her back up. Abigail giggled before answering. "Mavis had a surprise for her in the kitchen."

Collin threw open the kitchen doors, and the impact made the doors bounce off the stone wall. Mavis was lying in the middle of the kitchen floor, clutching her arm. "Oh God, no."

He ran out into the hall and grabbed someone standing close by. "Get Ian, and get a doctor, NOW!"

He returned to Mavis and slid down to his knees. "Mavis, what happened?"

"I fell."

Collin glanced past her to all of the red sauce and cheese covering the floor.

"Hang on, luv. The doctor is coming."

Mavis grabbed his lapel. "I had a vision, and it made me fall. Quinn's in trouble. You have to go to her. Go find Quinn."

"Where is she?" he asked, searching her gaze, wishing he could pull the answers faster from her lips.

"The old library. Look for the book with the black spine and white symbols. Find the book and find Quinn."

Ian busted into the kitchen with the McDougall doctor by his side, who ushered Collin out of the way.

"Ian, stay with Mavis."

Collin turned to leave, but Ian caught his arm. "What's going on?"

"The emerald is a fake, and Quinn is in trouble."

"Nay." Ian shook his head. "It bares the mark from the sword fight. I saw it with my own eyes. The one she returned was real."

"What are you talking about?" Collin lowered his voice and pulled him farther away from Mavis and the others in the room.

"Like the Menzies, the McDougalls have their tales. The emerald was a gift from my clan to yours. The McDougall laird at the time wanted to give the emerald as a wedding present and symbol of peace, but his heir did not. They battled over it. His son died from his wounds. That's how the curse started. His bride cursed the stone while clutching McDougall's dying body in her arms. It's believed she had gypsy blood in her. The emerald was damaged in the scuffle. The emerald Quinn brought you was real, Collin. I saw the mark. Now where's Quinn?"

His heart hammered against his ribs. "She's gone to find a killer. Stay here with Mavis and then send everyone home."

"Aye, go."

Collin rushed out of the kitchen and right into Ramsey. "Whoa, where are you going?"

"Quinn's in trouble."

"I should say so." His eyebrows dipped and his mouth turned down.

"She was going to the library. Never mind. Help Ian send everyone home." Collin didn't waste time explaining how Quinn could be in trouble in a library of all places. Hell, he didn't even know. He just knew he needed to get to her. Collin swallowed around the lump in his throat as he ran toward the east wing where all of the old books were kept. No wonder she said she'd planned to spend her day in the library. She was looking for something, and if his gut told him anything, he'd say she'd found whatever it was she was looking for.

Collin burst into the old library, expecting to find her, and God knows who else, but the room was empty. No sign she'd even been in the room. Had Mavis been wrong? Was she somewhere else? He hesitated to leave when he spotted the odd spine with symbols, not words, that Mavis had mentioned. If whatever she was looking for was in that book, there was no way he was leaving it behind.

He stomped to the bookshelf and pulled. He had heard a click before the book sprang back into place. The shelf pushed in, revealing a secret passageway that he hadn't even known was there. Collin stepped inside the dark corridor.

"Quinn," he yelled.

"In here." He heard her voice, and his heart skipped a beat as he stepped closer toward the sound.

A light was bouncing off the walls as she neared. "Don't let the door shut."

She said it a minute too late. Collin turned toward the click.

"Perfect." She sighed and shined the flashlight to a keyhole. "I don't suppose you brought a key?"

"Nay. What are you doing in here?"

"Following the clues. I found something interesting. You might want to come take a look."

She turned to leave, and Collin pulled her into his arms. "Wait. There's something I need to tell you."

"The emerald was stolen," she answered for him. "I know, but how did you know?"

"What do you mean you know?" he asked, releasing her arm.

"Because I found it...again." She grabbed Collin's hand and shined the light down the tunnel. Steel beams were secured into the rock leading him to believe they were for support from a possible cave-in. Every few feet more beams had been constructed, spaced to withstand the weight. He'd rounded a curve, and he could see the opening up ahead and the night sky outside. He was greeted by the sound of crashing waves in the distance, and his tense body slowly started to relax.

She bent down by the cave entrance and pulled back the red tartan. Beneath it was the emerald, along with several other Menzie heirloom pieces. "I found all these. Someone is stealing from you, Collin, and they're using this cave to smuggle things out."

"How did you figure this out?" Collin asked, picking up a jewel-encrusted box that had been among Gwinnie's things. He'd been told it had perished.

"In one of the paintings that Gwinnie's mother-in-law had commissioned, the psychic drew the book. This must be how they got the emerald out the first time."

"Looks like someone has taken to using it again." He rose and moved to the mouth of the cave. Waves were crashing against the shore ten feet below. There was no easy exit out of the place unless someone had climbing gear.

"Looks like they were using the ropes and that basket for lowering stuff down. It's kind of impressive. I doubt you'd see a thing from the castle windows." She picked up a rope lying against the wall.

Moonlight was dancing on the water. It would have been a beautiful place to be stranded, if the reason they were there hadn't been so wretched.

"How did you find me?" she asked.

"Mavis got hurt when she had a vision. She said you were in trouble and to look for the book that you described to her."

Quinn's hand flew to her cover her mouth. "Oh my God. Is she going to be okay?"

"Aye. She'll be fine, but your pizza dinnae fair so well."

Quinn's shoulders deflated as she leaned against his arm. "How long before someone finds us?"

Collin wrapped her in his arms and kissed her lips, the betrayal of the fake emerald replaced with dread. "Quinn, I need to get you out of here. If the person responsible comes back, there's no telling what they'll do."

She stepped out of his embrace. "Great. I don't suppose you can fly us out of here."

"Nay, but I can lower you down with the rope."

"I'm not leaving without you."

"You have to, luv. When you reach the bottom, you can get help and let me out."

She glanced down over the ledge and shook her head.

"You can do this, Quinn."

"I'm in a dress with heels, Collin. I can't do this."

"You can." He bent down to take off his boots and socks. "You can wear my boots for traction, and I'll lower you down slowly. I won't drop you. I promise."

"Collin…"

"Quinn, you're the strongest person I know. We'll do this nice and slow and get out of this together." He picked up the rope and tied it into a harness to ease her worry. He helped her into his boots and tied them as tightly as he could, so they wouldn't fall off her feet, before he helped her between the ropes. "I'll ease you down. Slow and steady."

She sat at the edge of the opening and waited until Collin had the rope around one of the beams to use as a makeshift pulley. He tied the other end around his waist. She would not be dying by his hands.

He pulled the tension from the rope and nodded.

Fear shined in her eyes. It was a look he'd never seen on her face, not even when knowing a killer was out to silence her. She eased over the rock, and he strained against the weight, trying hard to act strong when his insides just wanted to recoil. She let go of the edge and clung to the rope for dear life. Collin slowly lowered her, inch by agonizing inch. He took his time. "You okay?"

"Yeah," she hollered back. "The quicker I get down, the better. Just rip the Band-Aid already."

Collin smiled at her newfound resolve. His Quinn wanted to get down faster, so he moved a little quicker but watched for any problems she encountered. He had her about a foot above the ground when he heard the faint sound of a gun cocking.

"Drop the rope," Ramsey said.

Collin glanced down once more to find Quinn trying to get out of her harness. He threw the rope over. When it landed by her feet, her gaze shot up to the cave at the very second that Ramsey pulled the trigger.

The bullet seared his arm. The impact sent him back against the jagged stone wall and down to the cold floor.

KATE ALLENTON

Chapter 16

"No...oh God, no." Quinn kicked off Collin's boots and lifted her skirt to run along the base of the cliff, up the incline, and toward the driveway. The cars from earlier were gone. Only a few remained, along with an ambulance. Her lungs felt as though they were on fire before she reached the castle doors and burst through them right into Ian's arms.

He spun with her force. "Whoa there."

She slapped at his hands. "Let me go; let me go. Collin's been shot. I've got to save him."

"He'll kill me if I let you go running into harm's way. Where is he?"

Quinn blinked through the tears forming in her eyes as one slipped free. She didn't have time to explain. Fear knotted her insides as panic stabbed at her heart, twisting and turning, making it difficult to breathe.

"Let me go," she demanded through gritted teeth and wiggled free. Grabbing the hem of her skirt, she lifted it past her knees and ran, ignoring the questioning stares from the staff and lingering guests. She took the stairs two at a time. The sound of Ian's boots against the stone echoed behind her, but she wasn't stopping, not for him or for anyone. She ran into the old library and straight to the shelf. Grabbing a nearby chair, she pulled the book to open the secret passage and jammed the furniture in its way to keep it from closing. Ian stared, watching her, speechless.

"Well, don't just stand there. If this door closes, we'll be stuck," she said while climbing over the chair and into the cave. She paused. "If anyone comes out but Collin or me, then beat their ass."

She left Ian while he was demanding he be the one to charge in and she be the one to wait. Typical. Without the light, she slowly made her way in the dark around the corner to where Collin had been.

Collin's white shirt was covered in blood as he slumped against the cave floor. Ramsey stood above him with a gun pointed at Collin's chest.

Quinn slipped the dagger from the sheath and inched closer, hoping that Ramsey wouldn't hear or see her approach. Collin met her gaze, and his eyes widened, tipping Ramsey off to her presence, so she did the only thing she could. She stabbed him in the side with the sharp point of her dagger and dropped her shoulder, tackling him like she'd seen linebackers do on TV.

He hadn't expected the move and misfired, shooting the bullet into the cave walls. Ramsey pulled the dagger free and he dropped the gun to try and push her off. They both flew toward the cave entrance. Quinn was intent on making sure Ramsey never harmed another soul, and in that second, she knew she was going to die.

Ramsey latched onto her leg and was prepared to take her with him as he went out the opening. Her fingers caught the steel beam as she tried to hold up both of their weights. Her slick fingers were losing their grip as death knocked on her door. There were no flashes in her mind of events from her life. The anguish in Collin's gaze held her in a trance. She barely knew him, but she loved him, and she couldn't have picked a worse moment to figure it out.

"You willnae die."

He must have mistaken the look of confusion on her face for resignation to let go. Collin grabbed the gun and her arm at the same time. He fired a shot into Ramsey's body, and his weight instantly released.

"I've got you, Quinn."

She struggled to pull herself up, knowing his shoulder wouldn't hold out long. The pain alone could send him into unconsciousness, and then they'd both be screwed and sleeping with whatever animals filled the sea below. She crawled over the edge, thankful her dress didn't catch on the rocks, and pressed close to his side.

His face was pale and sweat covered his forehead as he held her gaze. His heartbeat was slowing as he battled to keep his eyes open. He tried to give her a reassuring smile.

"Collin Menzie, you better not die on me. Just hold on, baby. Please. Ian, help me," Quinn screamed, and within seconds, Ian crowded her, thrusting a flashlight into her hands.

"Collin, just hang in there." Ian hoisted Collin over his shoulder and carried him out of the secret cave and into the library.

Ian eased Collin down on one of the old couches. "You need to apply pressure while I go get my doctor."

"Hurry, please hurry." Quinn fought through the tears as she ripped her dress and pressed the fabric to his wound to staunch the blood flow.

Collin cried out in agony from the pain. He struggled to catch his breath before placing his hand over hers. "Quinn, you were so brave."

"Shut up. Don't you dare act like you're going anywhere."

His gaze softened as he reached up for her face and cupped her cheek. "You came back for me."

"You save me; I save you back. That's how we work."

"Aye. That's how we work."

Within minutes, the doctor was moving her out of the way as a stretcher and paramedics entered the room. Thank God, they were already here.

Quinn's stomach was tied in knots as they wheeled Collin from the room and into the waiting ambulance, where Mavis was already waiting. Quinn went to climb in, and the paramedic stopped her.

"There's no room."

"I'll bring Angus and her," Ian said. "We'll be right behind you."

Ian opened Angus' door and helped the frantic old man out from behind the wheel and then opened the back door for him, helping him inside.

Quinn ignored the gesture to climb in the back and jogged to the front passenger side.

"Let's go," she demanded and dove inside, shutting the door.

Angus leaned forward, holding out a handkerchief, and she took it. Her stomach clenched as she swallowed around the rock lodged in her throat. If Collin died, she'd figure out a way to bring Ramsey back from the dead, and kill him again. There was no way the evil bastard had survived that fall.

"He better be okay," she whispered as the tears started to flow.

Ian looked uneasy as he regarded her. She didn't have many breakdowns, but when she did, they weren't the sweet tears of a young girl. They were ugly, gut-wrenching cries that would leave her puffy and drained for days.

"Well, what do you know. The lass does bleed green." Ian started the engine, and if he hadn't been behind the wheel, she would have smacked him....hard.

"Ian, if you don't start driving, I'm going to know exactly what color it is that you bleed."

Chapter 17

Collin woke to Quinn's voice as she argued with Ian about leaving. He had no measure of time for how long he'd been out, but neither Quinn nor Ian was in their dance attire.

"You arenae doing him any good sitting by his side. Let Angus take you back to the castle to get some rest."

"No one asked you."

"Lassie, you're about to fall on your feet. Collin would want you to rest."

"Ian McDougall, don't make me hurt you."

"You cannae hurt me, Quinn. I'm no' wearing my kilt."

"I wouldnae test that theory, Ian," Collin said, turning both pairs of eyes to him.

Quinn's eyes were red and puffy, and Ian was right. She looked like she hadn't rested in days.

"Collin. Oh, thank God," Quinn said, moving to the bedside. She took his hand. "How do you feel?"

"Well rested, luv. Unlike you."

Quinn rolled her eyes. "Not you too."

"How long have I been out?" Collin asked Ian.

"Twenty-four hours. You lost a lot of blood, but they patched you up."

Collin's gaze softened as he stared up at Quinn. "And you've been here the whole time?"

"Aye, she has," Ian answered. "The staff tried to send her home, and she threatened bodily harm."

Quinn shrugged. "My court date is in two weeks."

Collin's mouth parted.

"She's teasin', Menzie. I talked them out of pressin' charges."

"I owe you." Collin smiled. "And Ramsey?"

They both shared a look. "He's dead. They found even more stuff at his house. We don't know how much he's smuggled out or where any of it went."

Collin let out an exasperated sigh. "I never would have suspected him."

"Well, the curse did say someone was going to die," Ian said, and Quinn smacked his arm.

"If I hear the word curse mentioned one more time, I think I'm going to scream."

Collin squeezed her hand, pulled her down, and kissed her lips. "I needed that."

"He's fine," Ian said and headed for the door. "Quinn, call me if you need anything. I'll convert you to red if it's the last thing I do."

"The hell you will," Collin argued, making Ian chuckle.

Quinn moved to the other side of the bed and crawled up against Collin, as he wrapped his good arm around her. She looked up at him. "I'm glad you're okay."

"I'm glad *you're* okay." He kissed her forehead and stroked her hair while she fell fast asleep.

Collin walked into the castle and was greeted by his staff. Each looked happy for his arrival, but none more so than Mavis, whose arm was in a sling. He crossed the room to her, lifted her good hand and kissed it. "We're both casualties of the curse."

"I cannae cook, but I can supervise."

Margarete headed for Collin, but Quinn quickly stepped in her way. "He's off-limits, and he needs his rest."

"You cannae talk to me that way."

"I just did, honey, so go back to playing with the furnishings because you won't be playing with him."

Collin wrapped his arm around Quinn's waist and kissed her neck. "Your claws are showing, luv. Why donae you take me upstairs and make good on the promise you made before the dance?"

She glanced over her shoulder and grinned. "I would, but I don't have my dagger."

"We'll make do." Collin took her hand and led her through the crowd and to the stairs. He had a date with this gorgeous woman and his bed. He wouldn't ravish her right away, but he could hold her in his arms while she got a decent night's sleep, and that was exactly what he did.

Collin woke before Quinn the next morning, partly because of the pain in his arm and partly because she was in his arms. Her time in Scotland was dwindling, and the thought made his heart ache. She had a life before him, one she'd be returning to. The curse had played out, well except the fire but with Ramsey no longer in the picture, the curse was all but over. A nobleman had indeed fallen, not only from stature but also from the side of a cliff to his death.

How had Collin been so blind not to realize what was happening?

"You're thinking too loud," Quinn mumbled, moving to rest her cheek on her hand.

"Sorry." Collin pressed a tender kiss to her lips. "I need to go down to my office and try to figure out what happened and take inventory of the missing items."

"I'm sorry your friend was a lowlife, sniveling thief."

Collin stroked her red silky hair. "It's no' your fault. You probably saved the castle and me from ruin."

"I save you; you save me. That's how we work." She grinned and slid out of the bed. "Is it safe for me to leave the castle?"

"Aye." Collin reached for her, and she scooted out of reach. "I need some more things from town and want to check in on Johnny. My sisters are going to want an update. I'm surprised they haven't shown up yet."

"Keep Angus with you, just in case."

She slipped into her jeans and fastened her bra before climbing back onto the bed, giving Collin a taste of her creamy flesh. "I'll be fine."

He cupped her cheek. "See that you are."

"I'll be back before you miss me." She got off the bed and slipped on her shirt.

"No' possible." He smiled up at her, and she frowned.

She stood at the end of the bed and whipped her hair up into a ponytail. "Collin Menzie. I love you. I didn't plan it and have no idea what to do about it, but I said it, so yeah."

She nodded, spun on her heels and left, leaving Collin speechless. The lass had stolen his breath, and then just disappeared in typical Quinn fashion. He rested his hands beneath his head as he repeated her words in his mind. She loved him. Surely he could convince her to stay.

Chapter 18

Quinn sat in the front passenger seat next to Angus. She no longer felt right sitting in the back, no matter how much Angus protested. Mavis and he weren't servants in the castle. They were Collin's family. "How's Mavis?"

"As bossy as ever," he answered with a twinkle in his eye. He reached over to the glove box, opened it and pulled out the replica emerald-encrusted dagger. "She wanted you to have hers."

"Oh, I couldn't." Quinn pushed his hand back.

"I'm no' telling her that. You can tell her, lass. I did my duty. She willnae be yelling at me. She can yell at you," he said, laying the dagger in her lap.

"Chicken," Quinn teased.

"No' chicken, smart." He tapped his head to point to his brain. "Where to first?"

"The hospital to check on Johnny."

Angus started the engine and glanced in Quinn's direction. "You still plan to leave?"

She nodded, remembering the bomb she'd dropped on Collin. "The sooner, the better."

"But, lass..."

"It's for the best." Quinn smiled, contradicting the ache in her chest. "I don't belong here, and he doesn't belong in Florida. There's no way to make it work."

"Forgive me for saying so, Quinn, but you're making a mistake."

A huge, colossal mistake, but then again, she never did anything small. She'd told him how she felt, which was more than she would have done a week ago. Like their attraction, she didn't fight it, and she didn't fight her newfound feelings, but acknowledging her feelings, and living the rest of her life in Scotland, were two very different things, and there was no way he'd ever be happy living anywhere else.

❖❖❖❖

Johnny was dressed, sitting in a chair, with a newspaper in his hands when Quinn walked into the room. She'd expected him to be covered in mountainous red bumps like a hormonal teenager, and yet, the few he had were covered in cream.

"They told me you weren't contagious anymore and you're healing in rapid time," she said, glancing around at his accommodations. It wasn't a five-star hotel, but it was better than the hotel where they'd been staying that first night.

"I'm glad you didn't come down with it."

"You and me both." Quinn walked over to the window and glanced down at the cobbled streets below. "When are they cutting you loose?"

"Tomorrow." Johnny folded the newspaper and rose. "I hope you're done with your business. I'd really like to go home and see my family. They've been worried sick."

Quinn clasped her fingers together instead of patting his arm. One couldn't be too careful. "I've finished my business, and I'm ready to leave when you are."

"Great." A smile stretched across his lips. "I'll call your cell when I get to the plane."

"Uh... My cell died a slow, painful death, and I don't have Collin's number at the castle. I'll call you when I head to the airport, and if you're not there yet, then I'll just wait."

A blush spread across Johnny's cheeks. "I'm sorry I delayed your return trip home."

"I'm not." Quinn did the unthinkable and squeezed his arm. "Well, I am sorry you got sick, but I'm not sorry I was stuck here longer than expected."

"Noon it is." He nodded. "If I have to sneak out of this place. I'll be there on time."

Quinn left Johnny's room and rubbed at her aching heart. She'd meant what she told Angus. She didn't belong in Scotland, but that didn't make it any easier. She'd miss this place. She'd miss Collin, Mavis, and Angus. Hell, she might even miss fighting with Ian. Nah. Who was she kidding?

Angus was waiting by the hospital entrance for her. The smile on his lips fell into a frown as she approached. "What is it, lassie? Did he take a turn for the worse?"

"No." Quinn linked her arm through his and led him outside. "Everything's fine. We're leaving tomorrow."

He patted her hand and opened the passenger door. "Everything will all work out. Have faith."

Faith. She had faith that she'd be leaving. She had faith that her sisters would give her an earful, and she had faith that there would always be ghosts and people who needed her help.

Quinn entered the castle with bags in both hands. She'd done more than purchase another set of clothes. She'd bought going-away gifts for everyone who had touched her life. She jogged upstairs and put most of them on the bed before jogging back downstairs and into the kitchen to find Mavis instructing a new person behind the stove.

Quinn's smile softened at the way Mavis gently guided the new woman, with words of encouragement. "I brought you a parting gift."

She turned to Quinn, her lips tilted in a frown. "You're leaving?"

Quinn gave her the best enthusiastic face she could muster and held out her bag. "One more day and you'll have me out of your hair."

Mavis' shoulders dropped as she took the bag. Reaching in with her good hand, she pulled out two objects wrapped in tissue. The first was her dagger.

"I gave this to you. Why are you givin' it back?" she asked, perplexed.

"Because it's your family heirloom. This dagger represents the strong women in your family. The ones the Menzies trust and that I trust. It's only right that it belongs to you and is passed down to the next generations."

Mavis pressed the treasure to her chest and smiled. "I'll make sure they know how the legend ends."

She unwrapped the second gift, and her eyes sparkled as she met Quinn's gaze. "Plane tickets?"

Quinn grinned. "Two open-ended round-trip plane tickets to Florida for you and Angus. You deserve a vacation, and I won't even expect you to come cook for me. Of course, you'll have to wait until after you teach your new student to cook. You can't leave Collin to go hungry."

Tears misted her eyes. "I've never been outside of Scotland."

Quinn winked. "I wish you the best that life has to offer, including amazing Italian food."

Quinn's heart clenched as she hugged her. She'd miss Mavis and her fabulous cookies. "Take care."

She hurried from the kitchen as her eyes misted. Quinn still had so much to do and pack, but she went in search of Collin. She found him in his office with a pile of paperwork up to his chest. He ran his hand through his hair as he read through some document. "I knew I'd find you here."

His gaze shot up, and the tension from his face softened as he rose. "It took you long enough. I thought I'd have to send out a search party."

"How bad is it?" Quinn asked, as she crossed the room toward him.

"It could be worse," he answered rounding the desk. He pulled her into his arms and lowered his head until his lips were a mere inch away from hers. "We should talk about this morning."

The butterflies, she'd always heard about, took to flight in her belly. The last thing she wanted to hear was if he loved her, or worse, that he didn't. "No, we don't."

Quinn pressed her lips to his to steal his train of thought. His hands on her back made a sensual path down her spine to her ass, and he lifted her in the air. She wrapped her legs around his waist and held on for dear life when he broke the kiss.

"I missed you, and I have something special planned for this evening."

"I'm leaving tomorrow," she blurted out and eased down his body. He remained quiet for several long seconds while she watched her words register. They'd both known the day would eventually come, no matter how hard leaving would be.

"Well then." He nodded and took her hand. "It's a good thing I planned your surprise for tonight."

He pulled Quinn out of the room and down the hall, bypassing the stairs where she thought their destination might lead. Taking her to bed apparently wasn't his idea of a surprise. Pity.

Quinn followed him through the kitchen and out into the courtyard where cell service was as dead as the ghost that hung out in the castle. To her surprise, they kept walking. Her hopes diminished when he turned away from the direction of the bridge and the empty cabin beyond the ridge.

Harness came running out of the barn, and she steeled herself for his attack. Instead, he wound his way around her legs and barked just as Garth, the lumberjack caretaker, walked Collin's stallion out of the barn by the reins.

"He's ready."

Collin grinned, climbed onto the horse and held out his hand. Quinn surprised them both when she took his hand and let him swing her up. He reached behind him for her hands and wound them around his waist. "Just hang on and I'll take care of the rest."

Quinn lowered her hands, stroking his jean-covered crotch. "We'll see who takes care of who."

Chapter 19

Collin slowed his horse over the ridge toward his favorite spot by the cliffs. The moon was high in the evening sky, and the stars twinkled in a cosmic dance. If tonight was her last night, he'd give her a night she'd always remember to replace the curse and the death.

Holding out his arm, he helped her down before dismounting.

"It's beautiful," she whispered into the night.

"It's my favorite spot." It was the perfect place for what he had to say.

He pulled her into his arms and kissed her with the passion of a warrior returning from battle. In some ways he was. The lass had crumbled every stone around his heart. She'd conquered the beast and given him back more than the emerald. She'd given him...hope.

Collin slowed the perusal of her tongue and kissed her tender lips, memorizing every detail about this moment and her.

"Stay with me, Quinn. Donae leave."

"Collin, I've got to go. I've put off my responsibilities long enough. It's time for me to get back to the real world and step out of the fantasy." She stared up into his eyes with a pleading gaze as if she truly wanted him to understand.

"I..."

She held her finger to his lips and quickly replaced them with her mouth. Her actions wouldn't silence him from what he had to say. Collin ran his fingers through her red hair and pulled the ponytail free as he kissed her. Her red tresses danced on the breeze, wild and untamed like the woman in his arms. Breaking the kiss, he rested his forehead against hers. "I love you."

She smiled up at him with sadness in her eyes. "Then show me."

"Aye. I plan to do just that." Collin slipped two blankets out of the saddlebag and laid them out on the ground, turning to find Quinn had already kicked off her shoes and was working the buttons on her blouse.

Collin stilled her hands and laid her down, covering her with his body. He kissed her lips and moved down her silky skin as he slid each button free. They had all night, and he planned to use every moment showing her exactly what she meant to him.

They lay naked beneath the moonlight, Quinn against his chest as he ran his fingers through her hair, their bodies only partially covered by the extra blanket. She raised her head and smiled up at him.

"This is perfect."

"You're perfect."

She ran her fingers over his chest, tracing the contours of his muscles and then laid her head back down. "I won't forget you."

"How could you?" He smiled down at her. "You're probably carrying my bairn."

Her chuckle rang out as she rolled off him. "Not likely, handsome. I'm on the pill, but if I ever have a kid, you'd be the front runner for baby daddy."

"Glad to know I'm in the running." Collin rolled and settled between her sweet thighs. "Maybe you need a reminder of what I have to offer."

"I think you're right."

Her smile brightened his world as her heels dug into his ass, pushing him into her sweet channel. He took his time pleasing her, searing this moment into her memory and his. Quinn Thatcher didn't know it yet, but her reluctance drove his determination. He'd let her leave, but never for good. This wasn't the end of them. There would never be an end if he had his say. It was just a matter of figuring out how to convince her to see things his way. No amount of water or distance could break the bond they were forming. She'd see it soon enough.

Her stomach grumbled as the hour passed, and he finally decided they both needed sustenance to maintain their strength. They were in for a long night, and the night was just beginning.

"It's time for food and part two of my plan." He slid the blanket free and slipped back into his clothes. As she dressed, he took his fill, memorizing her creamy flesh and planning to kiss every inch.

"You mean your plan didn't just include seducing me?"

'I think you were the seducer, luv." Collin winked, then packed up the blankets and mounted the horse. "I just picked the locale."

Collin led the horse in a walk to ease the tender flesh between her thighs.

They'd rounded the corner toward the castle when Quinn pointed to the sky. "Is that smoke?"

"Aye." Collin jabbed his heels into the horse, making Quinn's hold tighten around his waist. They broke through the clearing to find that it wasn't the castle on fire but the caretaker's house.

"Oh God," she whispered.

Garth stood outside swatting the flames with blankets as the horse jolted to a stop. Smoke rose into the night sky as flames grew. The air was thick with soot, covering the surrounding leaves. Collin helped her down and climbed off.

"Quinn, go alert the staff. They know what to do."

Collin yanked the blankets out of the satchel and doused them in the horse's water from the barn and returned to help in the battle.

Chapter 20

Quinn ran as fast as she could and burst into the kitchen to startle several people.

"Garth...fire." She'd no more said the words while trying to catch her breath than Mavis, Angus, and the staff flew past her. She'd turned to follow when a hand landed on her arm.

"No, Quinn. Help me get the extra extinguishers. They're in all of the second story rooms," Abigail said and led Quinn out of the kitchen and toward the stairs.

She raced behind her up the stairs toward her room, but Abigail disappeared into the door before Quinn's. She hurried inside, scanning the room in search of an extinguisher. The smell of kerosene made her nose twitch and pause. A pool of liquid sat on top of the dresser, and Quinn slid her finger through it and brought it up to her nose. She'd been right. Kerosene.

Quinn spun around to find Abigail standing in the doorway with a gun in her hand pointed at Quinn's chest. "You ruined everything."

She shook her head, not understanding Abigail's words. "What are you talking about?"

"You killed Ramsey. He was going to take me away from here with the money and treasures he stole."

Anger ripped through Quinn's body. This little bitch had been in on it. "You set the fire?"

A devious smile formed on Abigail's lips. "Garth was easy. He never suspected a thing. I knew Collin was going to take you to the cliff. It's where he took me."

Quinn swallowed hard around Abigail's lies. "He turned down Margarete. Why should I believe he'd ever love a sadistic bitch like you?"

Abigail pulled a lighter out of her pocket and flicked the Bic. "I hope you burn in hell."

"I'll be sure and save you a spot."

Abigail tossed the flame onto the kerosene-soaked dresser and eased out of the room, keeping the barrel of the gun trained on Quinn's chest. She pulled the door closed, and Quinn heard a lock click into place.

This wasn't happening. She wasn't dying in this room. She ran to the door and tried to turn the knob. It didn't budge. She covered her mouth with her shirt and hurried into the bathroom, looking for anything she could use to put out the fire. There was nothing.

Quinn ran to the window and pried it open, taking in a breath of fresh air. The fire at Garth's still raged on. She yelled, yet no one heard her voice.

Covering her mouth, she glanced furiously around the room. Her gaze landed on the bed and moved to the curtains. "I did it once. I can do it again."

She yanked the covers and the window linens free and made quick work tying them together. She had to get out before fire caught her makeshift rope on fire.

She tied one end to the steel bed frame and tossed the extra out of the window. Wrapping her arms around the linens, she climbed up onto the windowsill and eased herself out.

"Nice and slow." She replayed the words Collin had used and tried not to look down.

"Fire," she screamed at the top of her lungs as she held on for dear life and cleared the second story. If she fell now, at least she wouldn't die, but it would hurt like hell.

"Quinn." Collin's voice filled her with relief.

"There's a fire in my room," she hollered and eased another step down the wall. Her foot slipped, and she dangled, held by nothing more than the puny muscles in her arm. She screamed again.

"Quinn, let go. I'll catch you."

Sweat beaded her brow as she glanced down at him. He was still too far away. If he tried, he might miss.

White foam came pouring down on her from above. Someone was in the room putting out the fire. Thank God, the linens holding her life wouldn't burn.

Her arms burned as she hung on, trying to get another footing.

"Quinn, let go."

Quinn glanced down again to see a crowd had formed below. Abigail stood in the distance behind the crowd with a gun pointed directly at Quinn.

"Gun," Quinn screamed the moment the maid fired. A searing pain sliced through her ass. The sudden impact made her lose her grip, and she fell.

Collin caught her. How he'd managed with an injury himself was beyond her. They were both going to need a doctor. The crowd parted as he carried her through the courtyard. He paused at where Garth had Abigail restrained with her hands behind her back.

"Abigail was working with Ramsey, and she set Garth's place on fire in an attempt to keep everyone busy while she killed me," Quinn said as her vision blurred. No way was she passing out in front of them.

"Contain her and call the police. Have them charge her with arson and attempted murder."

He started walking past them, and Quinn glanced over his shoulder and hollered out, "Don't forget conspiracy to commit theft." Collin's face doubled before her eyes. "I'm about to pass out."

"I've got you, Quinn."

"You saved me." Her words came out a whisper before her world went dark.

Chapter 21

Collin held Quinn in the back of the car while Angus drove to the hospital. The front of his jeans was covered in blood from holding her in his lap, but he didn't care. He should have never let her out of his sight. He scooted out with her still in his arms. His own shirt was covered in blood from the stitches he'd torn catching her and carrying her, yet he pushed through the pain and walked with her in his arms directly into the emergency room.

The eyes of the nurse behind the counter widened as she hurried to open the restricted door to let them pass. She guided Collin to one of the rooms, where he carefully laid Quinn down on her side. "She was shot in the arse."

"Doctor," the nurse hollered as she left the room.

The next three hours passed as slow as molasses. Collin had spent the time being lectured about ruining his stitches as he was being patched up. He had sent Angus to the castle for fresh clothes and had changed. The rest of the time, he spent pacing in the waiting room.

He'd just changed when Ian showed up. He patted Collin's back and sat down beside him.

"Just say the word if you need me to come over and help protect Quinn."

Ian's words would have angered Collin any other day, but the truth was he was doing a poor job at keeping her safe. He'd been too caught up in the passion between them to even consider Ramsey had an accomplice.

"Abigail was working with Ramsey," Collin muttered and ran a hand through his hair.

"The maid?" he asked.

"Yeah. She burned down Garth's house and set Quinn's room on fire before locking her inside. Quinn escaped out the window."

"Good Lord, Collin. I don't know how you're going to talk Quinn into stayin' after all that."

"She already told me she's no'." His answer felt like a vise grip around his heart. "She's leaving in the morning."

"That's going to be one uncomfortable flight."

"Aye."

The doctor walked into the waiting room and lowered the mask covering his mouth.

"How is she?" Collin asked as his heart worked overtime thumping against his ribcage.

"She's fine. We've removed the bullet and stitched her up."

"Can I see her?"

"Sure. She's a little loopy from the drugs, but you can see her."

Collin followed the doctor down the hall and into recovery. Quinn was lying on her stomach. Her red hair covered the pillow.

"She shot me in the arse."

Collin's lips twisted into a smile at Quinn's attempted Scottish accent.

"That she did, luv."

"Scotland is just like flowers. They both want me to die."

"That wasnae Scotland, Quinn. That was Ramsey and Abigail. You cannae condemn a whole country for the actions of two crazy psychopaths. I bet you attract them everywhere you go."

"Don't forget the ghosts." She pointed to the empty corner of the room.

"Which ghosts came to visit?" Collin asked around his smile.

"All of them," she said, pointing again. "Redbeard, Ian's white-haired relative, Gwinnie." She paused and looked at Collin. "Who, by the way, was the one responsible for giving your emerald away to Clarence's ascendants. She was trying to help the poor." Quinn turned her gaze back to the corner. "Clarence, go sing your opera to someone else."

"Do you want me to call your pilot and delay your flight home?"

"Nooooo." Her eyes widened as she lifted her swaying head. "I have to goooo." She held out her hand and let it drop over the edge of the bed. "Collin, get me out of here."

"I cannae do that, Quinn, until the doctor releases you," Collin said, moving closer to her. He stroked her hair. "I'll get you to the airport. Just try and get some rest."

She nodded, and her eyes fell shut.

Collin spent the next hour in her room, sending away every bouquet that they attempted to deliver. He called Angus and had him inform the pilot what was going on in an attempt to explain to her family. The constable, also a friend of Collin's, had stopped by to take his statement about the fire and Abigail. He told Collin they'd found a storage unit that Ramsey was using to hide the stolen belongings.

The hospital released Quinn a few hours later, after she'd created a fuss and the drugs had left her system. Getting her home was somewhat of a challenge with her trying to sit. She ended up laying her head in Collin's lap while Angus drove.

His room and hers were filled with smoke from the fire and were being aired out, so they both stayed in one of the guestrooms on the first floor after she insisted on somewhere with an easier escape.

The morning would come early for both of them, so he held her in his arms all night long, unable to sleep. He listened to the sound of her breaths and stared at the ceiling. This wasn't how he'd envisioned their last night together.

"You're thinking too loud," she mumbled and lifted her head to look into his eyes.

"Sorry." He kissed her lips. "I was just thinking. Do you really have to go back?"

"Collin, we both know I do."

"Why? What is so pressing that you need to return? It's no' like we donae have ghosts in Scotland. You could stay here. Work from here, or hell, donae work at all. None of it matters except you and me being together. I love you, Quinn, and you love me too. That should mean something."

"It did. It does. I have to go back. I could never walk out on my family; I'm a partner for cripes sake; just like I could never ask you to abandon your home. Face it, Collin. We're from two very different worlds."

"Quinn, we can make it work. We've survived everything that was thrown at us. We can survive the small issue of distance."

"I have to go home." She rested her head against his chest.

"Will you come back?" Collin was almost afraid to ask, not wanting to hear her say no.

"I'll try."

Chapter 22

Quinn grimaced while staring into the airport bathroom mirror and swiped one more time to rid the smudged mascara from her red, swollen eyes and the tears started to pool again. How was it, after the long flight, that she had any tears left to shed? Saying goodbye to Collin had been hard. Seeing the disappointment on his face had made her feel like pond scum. She had to return, didn't she? Quinn knew the minute the plane took flight that she'd left her heart behind, and if her family didn't agree, they'd get over it.

Taking a deep breath, she stepped out of the bathroom and greeted Cara's and Becca's worried stares. Quinn headed directly into the line of fire, knowing their questions wouldn't wait. "I stopped a thief, scaled two walls, and got shot in the ass."

Their eyes widened in surprise, but she'd saved the best shocker for last.

"And I fell head over ass in love with a Highlander."

She loved that she could shock them into silence. She'd perfected it over the years. Quinn clapped her hands to get their brains functioning again. "Gird up, girls, and call our sisters back home. We have work to do. Linked Inc. is going international. Which one of you knows a good international attorney?"

They still stared, silently, as if her face was covered in green ooze and she was speaking in a foreign language.

Cara was the first to speak. "Wait, what? You fell in love?"

"Is that all you retained from everything I just said?"

She nodded, and Quinn smiled, letting her sister see the shine in her eyes. "I'm madly in love with Collin Menzie." Quinn grinned bigger. "I bleed green."

"Umm....I'm not sure that's possible," Becca said, tilting her head. "I'm pretty sure it's closer to a crimson color."

Yeah, okay. Quinn grabbed the handle

of her suitcase, wound her arm through Becca's and started toward the car.

A week later, eyeball deep in international paperwork, Quinn's eyes were starting to cross when a knock sounded on her office door. She glanced up to find her secretary with a package in her hand. "This was just delivered for you."

"Thanks." Quinn smiled, hoping the package was from their new international attorney.

The package was heavier than she expected. Quinn ripped it open to find a hardback book inside so she slipped it out. It was the sequel to the book she'd suggested to Garth, the Menzie's caretaker. She opened the cover to find an inscription on the first page.

An advanced copy for my pushy American friend. May the mystery, romance, and intrigue that I've written keep you entertained should you ever find yourself on a long flight back to Scotland.
Garth- "The Lumberjack."

Not much shocked Quinn in life, but Garth was the author of one of her favorite books! This was indeed a twisted world. Heat flooded her cheeks as a smile split her lips. She flipped the book over to the author's photo. It was the lumberjack, clean shaven and wearing a suit.

For two whole weeks, little trinkets started arriving at her office. Her lost dagger from Mavis, a package of cookies from Angus, and a red plaid bra from Ian with a note attached that said, *Red yet*?

No amount of Quinn's mother's nagging and bitching at dinner tonight could shake her resolve. Scotland called to her; going back wasn't a whim. She truly missed Collin.

"You're really doing this? You're willing to uproot your entire life and career over a guy?" Cara asked, leaning against Quinn's doorframe.

"I am," Quinn answered, signing the last document that would seal her fate. She shoved the paper inside an envelope to send to the attorney. "He's the one, Cara."

She smiled as an out of breath Rebecca ran into Quinn's office. "Quinn, I'm sorry to interrupt, but we have a situation."

Quinn slowly rose from her seat. "What?"

"Misty has a caller on the line who insists he has a curse and is demanding to speak with you."

A curse. Seriously? Quinn rounded her desk and stepped out into the call center, where all of the staff was working, some giving readings, some flipping tarot cards. It was just a typical day. Quinn spotted Misty across the room, standing in front of her computer, talking adamantly with her hands.

She looked relieved as she handed over her headset and stepped back to give Quinn room. Quinn slipped the headset on and cleared her throat. "Sir, we don't handle curses."

"Aye, so you've said, but I'm afraid I must insist." Collin's smooth baritone voice sounded like music to her ears, so she sat down in the chair and smiled.

"Is that so?" Her voice deepened to that of a phone sex operator.

"See, the thing is, my cook is psychic, and she's had a vision."

"Well, I'm sure the psychic cook can handle your curse problem."

"No, luv. See the portrait she painted depicting the curse isnae one that can be handled without your help."

Quinn leaned back in the chair and twirled her hair through her fingers. "You'll have to tell me exactly what's in this portrait."

"Turn around and find out."

Quinn spun in the chair to find Collin dressed in his sexy-ass kilt with a phone pressed against his ear, standing at the end of the row of cubicles. He was holding a portrait covered in brown paper.

Quinn tossed the headset onto the desk and sashayed toward him, unable to stop her grin. Ignoring the fact that he was holding whatever the painting was, she tossed her arms around his neck and kissed him with every bit of passion that had been building since the day she'd flown home.

Catcalls and cheers sounded throughout the room, but none of that mattered. She broke the kiss but kept her hold. "What are you doing here?"

"I came to bring you home, and there's this portrait business we need to discuss."

"Well then," Quinn said, pulling at the hem of her suit jacket and stepping back. "Business first and then pleasure. Lots and lots of pleasure."

His eyes twinkled with mischief. "Pleasure's gonna have to wait. We have dinner plans after business."

Quinn's brows dipped as she led him into her office and closed the door behind them. If she'd had blinds, she would have dropped them too. "You're not even in town for a day, and you've already made friends?"

"What can I say? I'm a likable guy."

"Yes, you are." Quinn crossed the room and cupped his cheek. "I've missed you."

He lowered his head and melded his mouth with hers before he broke the kiss. "Business first."

"Okay, show it to me. We handled the last curse. We can handle this one."

He lifted it into the chair, and with her stomach tied in knots, Quinn tore the paper off and stared with her mouth agape.

The painting depicted Collin standing behind Quinn while she held a baby swaddled in a green plaid blanket.

"It appears we're cursed to have bairns."

"Who?" Quinn shook the surprise from her head.

As if reading her thoughts, he answered, "Mavis painted it after another one of her visions."

"But I'm not...."

"Pregnant," he answered wrapping his arms around her waist. "No' yet." He placed a kiss on her neck. "Grab your purse. We're going to be late."

"Late, where?" she asked, grabbing her purse from the drawer.

"You'll see." He chuckled and led her out of the building, as if he'd been there a million times before, and into a waiting limo. She couldn't wipe the happiness from her face or ignore the fact that they were alone. She hiked her business skirt up and climbed into his lap. "I'm glad you're here."

"Me too. I figured I gave you enough time to miss me."

Laughter erupted from her lips. "If that were the case, you could have followed me home. I missed you before takeoff."

His hands trailed a path up her back and into her hair. He pulled the clip free, letting her red curls fall. "Dinner, then pleasure."

"Pleasure and then dinner," she corrected, unbuttoning the top button of her blouse.

"We're here." He redid the button and eased her off his lap. Quinn glanced out the window and up at the familiar three-story beach house.

"Why are we at my parents?" she asked, feeling a bit agitated that she had to share Collin with them so soon.

"I was invited to dinner," he answered, as if that explained everything. He slipped out of the limo and held out his hand. "I couldnae say no."

"Yes, yes, you could have." Her voice rose an octave as she took his hand and got out. "You aren't going to do something cliché like propose marriage in front of them, are you?"

He kissed her lips and whispered in her ear. "Worse."

He pulled Quinn to the door.

"Wait, what could be worse?" she asked as the door swung open. Ian was standing on the threshold in his kilt.

"There's my favorite American." He stepped out and crushed her in his arms, spinning her like a girl with a new doll.

"Put me down before I hurt you."

"That is no way to talk to our guests," Quinn's mother called out from behind the big brute.

"Sorry, Mom, but he's not a guest. He's a pain in my—"

"Quinn Elizabeth," her mother said, scolding her.

Quinn rolled her eyes as Ian lowered her to her feet and stepped out of the way for Collin and her to enter. The house was silent. She felt like a child about to give her first oral report. All eyes would be on her if Collin actually did what he said. She stepped into the large living room and froze. Every Scot she'd ever met was inside—Angus and Mavis, as well as other staff from the castle. Well, except the ones in jail or dead. Quinn's parents and sisters stood with hopeful looks on their faces, as though they were in on some big secret she'd been excluded from. Quinn turned to flee, and Collin's arm snaked around her waist.

"I told you she'd try and run," Cara said taking a twenty-dollar bill from Becca.

Collin led Quinn to the middle of the room. Heat flooded her face.

"You may think this is romantic, but it's not," she whispered.

"Aye. It will be." Collin dropped to his knee and held out the largest emerald ring she'd ever seen. "Quinn Thatcher."

"That better not be part of the cursed emerald."

"Aye, just a small part. I returned the rest to Ian. Now shut up and let me finish."

Quinn smiled down at him. Not many people would dare tell her to shut up, and she loved him for it.

"We thought you were returning something to us, but you stole something much more valuable."

"I did not," she quipped and glanced around the room at all the familiar faces.

"Aye. You did. You stole my heart." He rose to his feet. "You once told me that I save you, and you save me. That's why we work."

She stared up into the depths of Collin's eyes and could easily drown in the love that shined back. "That *is* why we work. I love you, Quinn Thatcher, and it's time you save me for good."

"Aww." Every female in the room gushed.

"Marry me, complete me, be my lady and my wife."

Her heart raced frantically against her chest. She always knew a moment like this would come. Maybe not with so many watching participants, but deep in her heart, she knew that this Highlander was her one.

"Aye," she answered.

Collin smiled in response and slipped the emerald onto her finger before kissing her in front of the roomful of people. They broke the kiss, and she held his gaze.

"What could be worse than this?" she whispered.

"You'll see." He winked before her sisters grabbed her arm to pull her from the room. "I'll see you in a little bit."

"Come on. It's time to get ready," Cara gushed.

Quinn was ushered up the staircase and gripped the rail when the vision of Collin hit her with the force of a punch to the throat. Collin was in a limo with Ian, both dressed in their kilts when an eighteen-wheeler blindsided the limo. "Oh God."

Panic and fear took her breath as she watched Ian and Collin close the front door.

She shoved off her sister's hold and ran down the stairs to throw the door open. They were already in the limo, and she raced to get in front of it. She slammed her hands on the hood and shook her head.

"Quinn, what are you doing?" her mother asked from the doorway.

"You can't go," she yelled as Collin stepped out of the car.

"I'll see you in a little bit, Quinn. Trust me."

She shook her head and rounded the car. "No, you can't go, please. Don't go." A tear slid down her cheek. She knew she wasn't saying this in a way for him to understand. She felt like she would faint. Her world was about to be ripped from her again, just like the first time. "Please don't go."

Collin pulled her against his chest, kissed her neck, and whispered in her ear. "What did you see?"

"An accident," she said with a shaky voice.

Quinn felt him nod against her head. "Then I willnae go." He cupped her cheeks and looked deeply into her eyes. "I willnae go. We'll just move the wedding here. I'm no' waiting another day to make you my wife, Quinn Thatcher. We'll just do it here."

"Wait, what?" His words were not making sense.

"We're getting married today," he answered. "It was a surprise. I wanted your family to witness, and I was going to let you plan a second one in Scotland."

"We don't have a license. We need a license."

"I took care of that," Cara said, stepping off the porch. "I just slipped it in some of the international paperwork that I had you sign." She glanced over her shoulder toward their parents. "Daddy called in a few favors too."

"We planned the decorations and banned the flowers," Becca said, winding her arms around their other two sisters, Grace and Harper.

"We brought the dress," Mavis and Angus announced, joining Quinn's sisters. "And the cake too."

"I brought the groom and your honeymoon attire," Ian announced.

"I'm wearing a suit." Garth grinned.

She'd never felt more loved than in that moment. So many people had cared enough to make this happen. She almost felt like a pansy for standing in the way of seeing all their hard work turned into a reality, but she'd rather be a pansy than left again with another fiancé to bury.

"I'm sorry. He can't go."

Her mother walked over to her and took her hands. "It's okay, dear. We'll fix everything and make it special."

"I don't need anything, Mom. I just need Collin, and that means he can't go."

"I know, and you'll have him." Her voice softened. "Now run upstairs and try on your dress. I'll fix everything."

Quinn let her mother lead her away and glanced over her shoulder. "You won't leave?"

"You have my word," he answered.

Chapter 23

Collin wrapped his arms around Quinn's waist and kissed her neck as a gentle beach breeze cooled the dancing guests.

"Lady Menzie," he whispered in her ear.

"Actually, I was thinking Thatcher-Menzie."

He chuckled. "Of course you were. I donae care what you call yourself as long as you call yourself my wife."

She turned in his arms and pressed her lips to his. "I can't believe you pulled all of this off."

"I'd move the heavens and earth for you." Collin turned her around to face the impromptu wedding. "Thank you for being my wife."

She glanced up at him. "Thank you for including my family, even if it was a little cheesy."

"Are you ready to find out what I'm wearing beneath my kilt?"

"I already got a glimpse thanks to the wind. I think my mom might have had a mini-stroke, and my sisters are green with envy." She grabbed his hand and led him back toward the house.

"You're a vixen." He chuckled and pulled her toward the house next door.

"Where are we going?" she asked, glancing back at the partiers.

"Our winter home," he answered and opened the back door, ushering her inside the three-story unfurnished home and straight to the only room with furniture. The bedroom. "I figured you probably donae want Margarete decorating it, so I saved that job for you. You can decorate it however you like."

"You bought a house...next to my parents."

"Aye, and as much as I love seeing you in my colors, Lady Menzie, I'd much rather see you wearing nothing but a smile."

Quinn grinned and slipped her zipper down, letting the dress pool at her feet. She stood naked except for the garter around her leg holding the emerald dagger. "I have a feeling you'll be making me smile for the rest of my life."

"Aye. It will be my mission to do just that."

ABOUT THE AUTHOR

Kate has lived in Florida for most of her entire life. She enjoys a quiet life with her husband and two kids.

Kate has pulled all-nighters finishing her favorite books and also writing them. She says she'll sleep when she's dead or when her muse stops singing off key.

She loves creating worlds full of suspense, secrets, hunky men, kick ass heroines, steamy sex and oh yeah the love of a lifetime. Not to mention an occasional ghost and other supernatural talents thrown into the mix.